UNSEEN ATTACKERS

The match burned Blacklaws' fingers. He dropped it and ground it out beneath his heel, turning slowly with the sensation of something wrong. He stepped back through the door, walked across the front room, and was nearly at this door when there came a grunting sound from outside.

He had no clear idea, in that first instant, of what came through the front door. It charged in with a coughing rush, knocking into him so hard he had to stumble backward to keep from falling. Then his foot caught on the rough cement floor, and he was thrown anyway. There was a thudding crash. The dim moonlight was shut off, leaving blackness thick as soot. At the same time a coughing shape crossed above him. Something smashed at his ribs with the beat of a triphammer. Blacklaws fired upward. Then his hand was knocked aside by a second grunting creature that plunged across him.

COPPER BLUFFS

LES SAVAGE, JR.

LEISURE BOOKS   NEW YORK CITY

A LEISURE BOOK®

January 1999

Published by special arrangement with Golden West Literary Agency.

Dorchester Publishing Co., Inc.
276 Fifth Avenue
New York, NY 10001

Originally published in a condensed version as "The Hide Rustlers" in *Zane Grey's Western Magazine,* 1950.

ISBN 0-8439-4478-1

Printed in the United States of America.

EDITOR'S NOTE

An earlier edition of this Western novel concerned with the hide trade in the Texas Gulf region appeared in a condensed magazine version in *Zane Grey's Western Magazine* under the title, "The Hide Rustlers." Certain scenes, vital to the author's intentions and a reader's understanding of the actions of the characters, were excised from this condensed version. Subsequently, a book version was published under the same title, but it retained the same editorial omissions. For this new edition, those scenes have been restored, based on the author's original typescript, so that now *Copper Bluffs* appears for the first time with the title and in the form the author originally intended.

COPPER BLUFFS

Chapter One

Kenny Blacklaws found the dead steer about four in the afternoon. It lay in a thick patch of winter-stripped brush about a mile from the Sabine River on the Texas side. Jefferson County was near enough to the Gulf to get its wind—a biting wind that whipped the brim of Blacklaws's hat against his face and made his black mare fiddlefoot nervously beneath him. When he swung off Tar Baby, she started to spook.

He checked the mare and stood against her with his hand on her neck, talking in a crooning voice. It was the habit of a lonely life and of a man who had a way with animals. The gentleness of it was in strange contrast to all the rough, masculine strength of his face and body. It soon quieted the mare, as it always did, and he hitched her to the brush down wind from the dead steer so the smell of blood would not excite her once more. Then he pulled his Bowie knife and walked over to the steer, grimacing faintly with his distaste for the job as he hunkered down to start skinning the carcass.

Doubled over that way, the tall length of him took on a heavier shape. Most of his weight was really in his chest and shoulders—a quilting of heavy muscles which filled his faded ducking jacket so completely that the seams spread whenever a turning motion put any strain on them. The bones of his face bore that heavy-framed strength, but they were set obliquely together, lending his cheeks and jaws a keen, sharpened look. There was a fine sculpturing to his mouth, with a latent humor curling at its tips. But that was spoiled by his eyes. They were recessed deeply beneath a sharply jutting brow. With his face in repose, they were filled with a darkness that seemed to come from a long time ago. It subdued the youth and humor of him, till he looked older than his twenty-six years.

His attention seemed to be on his job, but he remained acutely aware of each small sound that filled the desolate thickets about him. He let the corner of a glance now and then cross to the bindweed and *agrito* that lay in a matted tangle all about him. It gave a sense of spreading away from this clearing into an infinity, standing as high as a horse's withers in many places, broken on the horizon by small green islands of post oaks.

The black mare fretted restlessly, eyes rolling like white china toward the surrounding thickets as they rattled their winter skeletons in the wind. Blacklaws was about half way through his job when Tar Baby tossed her head and whinnied. He stopped working till he heard the distant popping crash, different from the rattle of wind. He felt the impulse to rise and stopped himself with difficulty. This was what he wanted, wasn't it? *I've skinned enough animals now*, he thought. *I've left my trail open for whoever wants to follow. It's about time somebody came.*

He was still peeling off the tough hide when the three horsemen threaded their way from the thicket. The man in the lead sat his short-coupled billy horse in the ostentatious seat a heavy-gutted man so often adopted.

The immense girth of him made Blacklaws's big frame look small. He was hatless, his bald head shaped like a bullet, the flesh turned a luminous yellow in the pearly light of the sunless afternoon. His eyelids were merely creases in the pawky pouches of fat that contained his eyes. He reined in his billy horse and sat, leaning heavily into the cantle, stirrups flapped out wide, staring with that carnal grin Blacklaws remembered so well.

"Heard you was back, Kenny," he said at last. "Wouldn't have recognized you. They must feed well up north. You've filled out as all hell."

Blacklaws had come to his feet, and he returned the man's grin. It spread outward into his face, deepening the wind tracks in his bronze cheeks and drawing together the fine-grained network of wrinkles about his faintly squinting eyes. On the surface, it gave his face all the youth and humor it should show. Yet there was still something reserved about his eyes, holding all the humor of his grin ironically within himself, projecting none of it to the heavy man.

"Nine years changes a man, Roman," he said.

John Roman's grin broadened. "It does, Kenny. It does. Folks wondered why you left. Now they'll be wondering why you came back."

Blacklaws was still smiling. "Do you wonder, Roman?"

The other man stared at him a moment longer then threw his head back in a surprising burst of laughter—guttural and explosive with all the untrammeled forces of him. "I never wondered why you lit a shuck, Kenny. I would have run away long before you did. I never saw

11

a man treat his boy the way your father treated you."

At last the smile fled Blacklaws's face. "Not my father."

Roman sobered abruptly too. "My apologies, Kenny. Your *stepfather*. I guess you *would* be touchy about that. You picked a poor time to leave the country, though, Kenny, the same day he was killed. There was a lot of talk."

Something dogged entered the shape of Blacklaws's mouth. "Did it come to anything?"

Roman shrugged. "Most folks wouldn't have blamed you if you had killed Martin Garland." He paused, studying Blacklaws. "Did you . . . Kenny?"

Blacklaws's face had been young there for a space, while he was smiling, but now his eyes held that somber darkness once more. "Do you think I'd come back if I had?"

Roman's chuckle was the scrape of a rusty saw. "I guess not, Kenny."

The other two men had not spoken, holding their fiddling horses in subservient silence to John Roman. Blacklaws's attention came momentarily to them now. He knew Agate Ayers, a tall alley cat of a man, with hemp for hair and saddle leather for skin. His narrow shoulders were carried in a perpetual stoop, lending a deep concavity to his chest, giving accent to the pear-shaped curve of his little potbelly that thrust itself against the beltless waistband of his Levi's.

The other man was new to Blacklaws. He rode a black horse with a coat so slick the dampness of this fog lent it a glossy sheen. His clothes, too, were an unrelieved black. There was something Creole to the way he clubbed his long hair at the base of his neck and to his depthless black eyes, holding Blacklaws in an unwinking stare.

"That's Gauche Sallier, Kenny," Roman said. "He

used to punch cattle on the Louisiana side.''

Blacklaws looked at the man's feminine hands, the flesh unmarred by any rope scars. ''That must have been a long time ago,'' he said.

Sallier made some sharp movement in the saddle, but Roman's voice halted it.

''Take it easy, Gauche. Kenny's a man who can read sign like an Indian. It was just an observation.'' He looked down at Blacklaws. ''You don't want to aggravate Gauche, Kenny. He's touchy as a steer with heel flies.'' There was another pause and then Roman asked: ''Why did you come back, Kenny?''

''Man's rope frays out sometimes, Roman.''

''You would have done better to let it fray out up north,'' Roman said. ''Didn't they tell you about the skinning war that's going on down here? Meat don't bring enough money in the northern markets to make a drive worth-while, and nobody's buying cattle in Texas. All a steer's good for is its hide and horns. The only big operators that have managed to keep their heads above water are the ones that sell the hides and pack their own meat.''

''They told me all about that,'' Blacklaws answered. ''They told me hides down here are just like mavericks used to be. The skin of a dead cow belongs to whoever finds it.''

''Only hide rustlers have been taking advantage of that custom and killing any cow they come across for its hide,'' Roman said. ''Everybody who don't own any beef is out slaughtering somebody else's for the hides. It's driving out what big operators are left.'' He grasped the horn of his saddle, squeezing it till the great cords in his wrist popped faintly. ''It isn't driving me out, Kenny. Nobody's taking the hides off my cattle, dead or alive. You must have known this was one of my Double Sickle steers, but I'll let it pass this time. You're

13

fresh back and didn't know how things stood. I'll give you this warning now. Don't ever let me catch you taking a Double Sickle hide again.''

"I always observe the customs of the country, Roman.''

Roman's eyes squinted almost shut. "What does that mean?''

Blacklaws made a solid figure there, with the wind ruffling the edges of his ducking jacket against his big torso. "I came back looking to keep from starving to death, Roman. I was willing to work at anything I knew. But there wasn't anything. A little man's got to exist, same as a big one. Hides are selling for fifty cents apiece in Galveston, and King Wallace told me he'd haul whatever hides I got whenever he went down there. I'll leave your live steers alone. But it's still not thought dishonest to take a hide off a dead steer.''

Roman reacted with some vicious shift in the saddle. Then he halted that, as if restraining himself, and settled heavily back into leather.

"Not my hides, Kenny. Hand this one up.''

The wind caught Blacklaws's hat in a new blast, whipping the brim against his face. "No, Roman. I skinned this hide. I'll keep it.''

Roman spoke heavily. "Gauche, climb down and get that hide.''

The Creole slid off his horse without any lost effort. He dropped the reins over the black's head and then handed them back up to Agate without looking at the man. His eyes were turgid as ink, holding Blacklaws's gaze. The dim illumination filling the brush cast little shadow, leaving only a faint stain in the waxen texture of flesh beneath Sallier's sharp cheekbones.

"Will you give me the hide, *m'sieu*?'' he asked.

"No,'' Blacklaws said.

"Will you step back, then, and let me pick it up?''

14

"No."

There was another moment drained of sound and movement. Without taking his gaze from the Creole, Blacklaws saw how avid the light in Roman's eyes had become. He knew Roman and Agate meant to back up Sallier, if the Creole could not do it alone.

"Very well, *m'sieu*," said Sallier.

He moved forward, bending casually to reach for the hide. Blacklaws lunged at him. The Creole's instant reaction revealed he had been expecting this. But he had not counted on so much speed from such a heavy man and did not jump far or fast enough.

Blacklaws caught the left-handed man before his gun was completely out. He clutched Sallier's free right arm and swung him off balance and then pulled him around in a whipping half circle. When the arc was completed, Sallier stood with his back in against Blacklaws and his freed gun pointed helplessly at Roman.

At the same time Agate Ayers dropped the reins of the black and Roman tugged his bearskin coat aside to go for his own gun. With Sallier against him, Blacklaws caught that gun arm down at the wrist. Sallier gave a vicious heave, trying to tear loose, but Blacklaws twisted his arm so hard he dropped the gun with a cry of pain. Then Blacklaws put the flat of his hand against the Creole's back and gave him a heaving shove.

The man staggered heavily forward to keep from falling and could not help plunging into Roman's horse. The beast whinnied shrilly and reared up. Roman had to forget about his gun to fight the animal. His reining pirouetted the beast around to smash against Agate's horse.

Before they got control of their animals, Blacklaws picked up Sallier's gun. Roman finally got his billy horse back down, and Agate managed to quiet his dun. His gun was out, and he wheeled the animal back but, when he saw the weapon in Blacklaws's hand, he stopped. He had a twangy, nasal voice.

"Ain't that a sack of hell," he said.

Blacklaws said nothing, standing heavily there until Agate slipped his gun back into its holster. Sallier wheeled to face Blacklaws, rage making its whitened stamp on his face and causing his voice to tremble.

"You should not have done that, *m'sieu*," he barely whispered.

Blacklaws ignored him, watching Roman. "Don't ever put your heel-dogs on me that way again," he told the man.

Roman's own anger mottled his face with diffused blood. He settled his weight in the saddle like a sulking steer, the breath leaving his nostrils with a wheezing sound. Finally he got himself under control. Puzzlement robbed him of some of the anger.

"You don't seem very mad, Kenny," he frowned.

Blacklaws laughed suddenly. It made his face look young again. He tossed Sallier's gun to the man's feet.

"You'll never make me mad, Roman," he said. "But you'll never do anything like this again and get off so easy, either. Now go on back to your hide factory. This skin's mine, and I'm keeping it."

Chapter Two

After the three men had left, Blacklaws stood in the deepening twilight, listening to the rustle of their passage out through the thickets fade and die. The wind was whipping more vindictively at his hat brim, stinging his cheeks, and drawing his eyes closed till they were barely slits. *They didn't make me mad.* That kept going through him triumphantly. *They tried like hell, and they didn't make me mad.*

Finally he turned to finish skinning the carcass. Then he lashed it on back of his saddle, mounted, and reined the animal back toward the Sabine. He found the river road and followed it southward. Behind him about four miles was the town of Copper Bluffs and before him was the Manatte plantation—or what was left of it.

Where the long drive entered the river road, he pulled up. The house was out of sight, hidden in the grove of post oaks, but he could remember too well what it looked like, with its slender colonnettes and its long gallery set high on brick piers. And he could remember Corsica, standing on that gallery, waiting for him. . . .

He blocked off his impulse to turn in, glancing down at his blood-grimed hands and dirty clothes. He could not see her in this condition—after so many years. He gigged Tar Baby on southward, topping bluffs that overlooked the twisting river, black and silken in the failing light. But he was still thinking of Corsica Manatte, admitting to himself that his reluctance to see her went deeper than his present appearance. It went back nine years and stopped in a dank bayou somewhere west of the river. He wondered if Corsica had heard the talk, too. Undoubtedly. And it would be lying between them whenever they met, putting a blight on their meeting. It was what really had kept him from calling on her.

Six miles south of the Manatte house he turned off the road onto an old cattle trail that dipped immediately into the woolly dusk that filled a dense stand of loblolly pine and chinquapin. These thinned out into a broad prairie thick with saw-bladed salt grass. He slopped through stagnant water which pooled the low points, salty enough to leave deposits of brine at its edges that held a luminous gleam in the last light of day.

He heard the Smoky Cranes before he saw them, whipped by the wind till they slashed at each other like sabers, setting up an unholy clatter that ran through the timber with a sound like the clash of armies in battle. He trotted through the last stand of post oaks, ducking grapevines that hung from the trees in loops thick as a man's wrist, and broke into a clearing by this canebrake where the old, crumbling shack cabin stood.

He unsaddled his horse and put it in the pen and carried his rigging around to the front. Weariness had robbed him of his usual caution until now, but as he stepped around the corner his eyes automatically picked up the fresh signs about the door. This halted him, put him back around the corner of the shack. He lowered his saddle to the ground and then stood with his back against the unpeeled logs, hand on his gun. There were no hoofprints. That meant the man had hidden his horse in the canes or the timber. And there had been no attempt to erase the bootprints. The heels had been flat. That excluded a cattleman.

"Carew?" he called softly.

"Never mind, Kenny boy," answered a man from within the shack. "I ain't staked out to cut you down."

Blacklaws swung around the corner and to the door, pushing it open and going through and then taking a step aside so he would not be skylighted. Charlie Carew's boots scraped softly against the puncheon floor. The hurricane lamp clinked as he lifted its top, struck a match.

The lamp flared into life, its saffron glow stamping Carew's face against the darkness in a bold intaglio. He sat in the only chair in the room, a paunchy man in a rumpled frock coat and frayed broadcloth pants. His stovepipe hat lay on the table, and his thinning hair was combed carefully across the protuberant bulge of his head. A sly judgment of everything within their vision glowed from his small eyes, deeply recessed beneath his hairless brows.

"How did you know it would be me?" he asked.

Blacklaws moved over to the Dutch oven, squatted down to lift a length of cottonwood from a pile beside it, stirring the ashes level before he put it in. Then he got kindling, planted it, and started his fire.

"You were the one who wrote the letter to Laramie Grange," he said. "I figured you'd be the one to meet me here. When you didn't show up right away, I supposed you wanted it secret. So I didn't look you up."

Carew pulled a cigar butt from his pocket, already chewed into a blackened and pulpy stub. He took his penknife out and opened it, carefully pared the end off the cigar, thrust it into his mouth, and began chewing complacently on it.

"Always figuring things out, ain't you, Kenny? I never saw such a man. All right. Here's why I didn't want anybody knowing you were hooked up with me. We're up against it. Under ordinary conditions, with beef selling at decent prices, that custom of a dead cow's hide belonging to the man who finds it is all right. But when the hide is the only thing left that's worth any money, the result is pretty obvious. They used to rustle cattle. Now they're rustling hides. Most of the rustlers are working alone or in small bunches. But here in Jefferson County. . . ."

"You've got an organization," supplied Blacklaws.

"That's a mortal fact. I guess you've been around long enough to pick up the details. This organized bunch is the one that's driving the Jefferson Cattle Association crazy. If they keep on, they'll have every big operator in the county out of business. The worst of it is they've got a packery of their own hidden somewhere. It allows them to handle the cattle in any numbers they want. Instead of killing the cows where they find them and skinning them on the spot, they can drive a big cut to their packery and skin them at their leisure."

Blacklaws rose from the fire, shrugging out of his ducking jacket, and turned to hang it on a peg. "And you haven't been able to locate this hidden packery?"

"A mortal fact. That's what we want you to do, Kenny. You know how much of the Big Thicket has never been seen by white men. You know there isn't anybody who's been through Congo Bog. There's an awful lot of this country that isn't known."

"They've still got to ship the hides out. Have you watched the coast?"

"Like a hawk. The only ones shipping out that way are John Roman due south of here and Allen and Poole way over on Galveston Island." Carew chewed meditatively on his cigar, studying Blacklaws. "My men and I are too well known around here to get any place. In fact, anybody remotely connected with the law is pegged the minute he starts to work in this country. You're our last bet. You know the country, the people. Yet you've been away long enough to have no known connection with any particular faction. Last but not least, we know how good the work was you were doing for the Laramie Grange Association up in Wyoming.''

"We?"

Carew tilted back in the chair, chuckling. "Don't worry. None of the cattlemen in the Jefferson Association knows why you're back. There are about six stock detectives working for the association now. I run the department. I'm the only one who knows about your undercover work for Laramie Grange, or who knows why you're here.''

"John Roman doesn't know, then?''

The man's chuckle shook his pouchy belly. "Not a bit of it. I hear you had a run-in with him today.''

"You've really got your lines out.''

"I came across Roman on the trail. You must have gone right to work.''

Something was shaping obscurely in Blacklaws's face as he stared into the flames. "It took me a couple of days to see how things stood. I could guess just about what you'd want me to do. If it got around that I was rustling a few hides on my own, there would be less suspicion that I was connected with you. It might even get me into the confidence of other rustlers.''

Carew chewed industriously at his stogie. "Haven't changed a bit, have you? Always figuring things out. Even as a kid. Always something working in that mind.'' He grunted. "You achieved your purpose, anyway. Roman is already thinking of you as a hide rustler. It will get around.'' Carew tilted his chair back farther, squinting at the murky expression on Blacklaws's face. "Something you want to ask me about?''

"In your letter, you mentioned the Manattes,'' Blacklaws said.

"I thought that would help bring you back. You still in love with Corsica?''

21

"I was only seventeen when I left. A kid that age doesn't know what he feels."

"And yet part of the reason you came back was for her. You think she's in trouble, and you want to help her."

"You implied they were mixed in this somehow."

"Phil Manatte's doing something," murmured Carew. "I don't know what yet. But he's mixed up in something."

Blacklaws frowned. "I can't believe Corsica would have anything to do with it."

"People do strange things when their backs are up against the wall." Carew grinned suddenly, peering intently at Blacklaws. "Maybe she was the *whole* reason you came back."

This brought Blacklaws around to face the man. The raw, bleak expression in his face was plain now. Neither man spoke, and the silence gained cottony substance in the dusky room.

"Roman said they couldn't make you mad," Carew murmured at last. "Said another man would have been swelled up like a poisoned pup, but you was just grinning like a Cheshire. Now why can't you do that for me?"

Blacklaws did not reply. His chin tilted slightly. It changed the shadows on his face, turning the eye sockets to sooty pools from which the whites of his eyes gleamed as enigmatically as marble. Carew's teeth clamped down on the cigar.

"I thought something more than the Manattes was on your mind, Kenny."

"Don't cat-and-mouse me, Carew," Blacklaws said in a strained voice.

Carew sighed heavily, dropping the chair back down to its front legs and planting his feet solidly on the floor. "All right. What would you like to know?"

"Your letter was very cleverly worded, Carew. The president of Laramie Grange wanted to know what Martin Garland's death had to do with the hide rustling."

Carew grinned faintly. "Nothing. You know I put that in there for you alone. I said we'd found out who murdered Martin Garland. I thought that would bring you back. Your foster father had a lot of enemies. When he was killed out there in Bayou Lafitte, it didn't cause much sorrow. But the fact that you disappeared the same night made a lot of talk. There was no proof, so that died down. Then this hide rustling broke out. We combed things pretty fine, Kenny. A lot of funny clues have popped up. First it was Martin Garland's bullwhip which had disappeared at the time of his death. Then it was a man who had seen Martin Garland killed."

All the breath seemed to leave Blacklaws's body. "Who?"

Carew removed the cigar absently from his mouth. Then he glanced at it, and a disgusted snort fluttered his bulbous nose. He flung the butt from him.

"Damn' things," he muttered. "Think I was a cow or something, chewing my cud." He wiped the back of his hand across his mouth. Then he settled a little in the chair. "It doesn't actually matter to me just who killed Martin Garland. Personally, I guess I hated him as much as the next man, and I'd say good riddance. On the other hand"—the chair creaked beneath his small shift—"we need this job done. You're about our last bet. So look at it this way. We have no official interest in the death of Martin Garland. Do this job, and we'll forget what we found out."

"And if I don't do the job?"

Carew looked uncomfortable. "You must have known the answer to that, Kenny, or you wouldn't have come back. I guess you know your stepbrother is practicing law in Copper Bluffs now. If Quintin Garland ever got

23

his hands on evidence proving who killed his father, he wouldn't quit till he had the man hanged, Kenny.'' Carew's eyes squinted slyly. ''Especially if he had hated that man to begin with.''

The light caught a savage flash in Blacklaws's eyes, and his body jerked sharply with an impulse he could not abort. Carew straightened in the chair, one hand darting out to grasp the edge of the table.

''Won't do you any good to get mad, Kenny.''

Blacklaws continued to look at him a moment. Then he turned away from the man, facing the fire.

''Get out,'' he said.

Carew's boots scraped the floor as he rose. ''I thought you were the one who couldn't be prodded, Kenny.''

I'm not mad, Blacklaws thought savagely. *You can't make me mad.* ''Just get out,'' he said.

The puncheons shook with Carew's ambling passage to the door. Opening it, he paused again. ''I'll be around in about a week, Kenny. I'll want some kind of word then. And I hope you aren't planning on quitting the job so soon. It would be the second big mistake of your life.''

Again Blacklaws did not answer. He heard the man turn and go out. When he finally lifted his face, there was a whipped look to it. And all he could seem to think of were Carew's words: *If Quintin Garland ever got his hands on evidence proving who killed his father, he wouldn't quit till he had the man hanged, Kenny.*

Chapter Three

Quintin Garland stood dismally at the window of his law office in the French House, looking out over Copper Bluffs, a bitter frustration robbing his mind of any directed thought. Absently his eyes found the jetties, thrusting their rotten pilings out into the Sabine below the bluffs, as if to snag what meager river traffic remained to this forgotten town. From here, the river road shelved its treacherous and crumbling path up the face of the coppery clay bluffs to the first buildings of town.

The fog banks crawled up this road, rising from the river to twist through the town in oppressive layers, rent here and there by the passage of a forlorn rider or a heavy freight wagon laboring through the muck. The somber mood filled Garland darkly, turning his mind to the defeat, the bitterness this town had brought him in the last five years.

He was a tall man, narrow without being thin, a sense of tensile strength to the keen line of his body in its dark broadcloth. His hair was the color of amber, changing hues when the slightest motion of his head shifted the light upon it. There was a peak to his brows that lent his aquiline face a sardonic look, and there was the restless quest of a hunting hawk in his deep-set eyes.

"Brooding again, Quintin?"

The lawyer wheeled sharply. He had not heard anyone enter. The door was open, however, and the woman stood there, regarding him from those great solemn eyes that had always disturbed him so. She made a tall, roundly formed shape in the rectangle of the door, a pork-pie hat set jauntily on her abundant black hair, the uplifted depth of her breasts pushing insistently against the lapels of her dark coat. The dim light of the room turned the texture of her flesh to satin and lent a dusky sensuality to the ripeness of her lips. Her face held a broad, strong beauty through the cheekbones, but they were set high and slanted sharply inward, so that the faint shadows lying obliquely beneath them, for Garland, had always given her features a faintly Oriental cast.

"You didn't tell me you'd be in town today, Corsica," Quintin Garland said.

Corsica Manatte smiled. "Dee drove me in. We were looking for Phil to be back from Houston today. I guess he's been delayed." The smile faded, and she moved impulsively toward him. "You shouldn't let the outcome of the trial depress you so, Quintin. You did your best. I was surprised at such a hard decision."

"Decision, decision," Quintin said in a burst of savagery. He wheeled away from her to stalk across the room to his desk. "The jury didn't make any decision. They knew how they were going to rule before the judge sat down. The foreman of the jury used to work for Roman."

"But you still have no reason. . . ."

"No reason to what?" he said, wheeling on her. "Roman's out to break me, can't you see that? Jesse Tanner shot that Obermeier rider in self-defense. Just because they found Jesse with a few Obermeier hides. . . ."

She shook her head. "All you had was Jesse Tanner's word that the Obermeier rider drew before he did. And the court proved definitely that Jesse had taken those hides from freshly killed steers."

"That's the point. The only issue was rustling. In any

other court they would have dropped the murder count. It was a clear case of self-defense. . . .''

"It wasn't clear. If Jesse hadn't been rustling, his word that the Obermeier rider drew first might have stood. But as the prosecutor said, the attendant circumstances were so damning . . . !''

"Obermeier would do well to have *you* prosecute the next case."

A hurt look darkened her eyes. "Quintin, don't be like that."

He shook his head, turning partly away from her. "I can't help it, Corsica. If you've lost faith in me too, I don't have anything left. Lisa Peddigrew withdrew her retainer after the trial. All the people I've fought for are losing confidence in me. Can't you see what Roman's doing? This is the sixth case I've lost in three months . . . ?''

He trailed off at the confused shock in her widening eyes. "A man's going to be hanged," she said. "They're building the gallows for Jesse Tanner right now. And all you can think of is that you've lost another case."

The bitterness washed from his face, leaving it sober and contrite, and he went over and caught her by the elbows, speaking intensely. "Forgive me, Corsica. You're right. My failure is so insignificant beside the main issue. It was blind of me."

She held back from him, studying his face. "Quintin, when you first came back from Austin and said you'd decided to give up that wonderful job because you thought the little men needed you more back here, I was so proud of you. The small operators have needed a champion for so long, with Roman and Sharp and Obermeier in control. But now. . . ."

He waited for her to finish and, when she didn't, he asked: "Now . . . what?"

27

She seemed to lift against him, almost whispering it. "Make me stay proud of you, Quintin."

It brought one of his rare smiles, transforming his face for that moment, erasing the hungry hollows beneath his cheeks and robbing his eyes of their sharpness. She responded to it, as she always had. Her breasts lifted and swelled with a deep breath. Her lips parted. He pulled her tight and kissed her. But even as he did so, he felt the change run through her. Some of the eagerness seemed to leave the lips, and they lost tension beneath his. He took his mouth off and held her away from him.

"Losing my touch?"

"Of course not, Quintin."

"What is it?"

She pulled gently free, turned to walk to the window, stood there looking out a minute. Then she faced back to him. "I had something in my mind when I came up. It was driven out by that talk of the trial. It came back just then."

"What?"

"Quintin . . . ,"—she hesitated, her face darkening, then almost forced herself on—"Quintin, did you know that Kenny Blacklaws is back?"

He could not hide his reaction to that. The surprise of it left his mind blank. He felt the blood drain from his face. A pulse seemed to break out in his temple. Then the first blankness was gone, and he turned away so that she could not see the depths of his feeling. He walked to the desk, taking hold of its edge in the irrelevant need to get his hands on something. Finally he spoke, low and gutturally, almost to himself.

"Why should he be back? Why?"

The throaty tones of her voice condemned him. "You can't still hate him that much."

"Why not?" he said bitterly.

"Because nobody else disliked him. Not many people

28

understood him, but nobody disliked him. Why were you two always fighting?''

"We lived together thirteen years," he said. "Isn't that enough?"

"No," she said. "Not for feeling this way."

"I've got my reasons," he said.

"What reasons?"

"Why do you ask it that way?" he inquired.

"What way?"

"As if you already know."

She shook her head impatiently. "I don't know what you're talking about. If you have reasons for hating Kenny so, haven't I a right to know them?"

"You wouldn't want to know," he said. "It's between Blacklaws and me, that's all."

"If he couldn't make out up north, he has as much right here as you," she said.

Garland turned to face her. "How can you stand up for him?"

"I'm not standing up for him," she said heatedly. "Every time I try to take a decent, adult view of things, you accuse me of turning against you."

"Then why can't you see what he's doing? He knows I'm here. He knows the two of us can't stay in the same town. He had the whole world. Why should it be here . . . ?"

The expression of her face stopped him. "I think I'd better go, Quintin," she told him, turning away.

He reached out for her. "Corsica. . . ."

"No," she said. "I think I'd better go."

He stood at the window after she left. He could not see the street below. He could not even feel the depression he should at fighting with Corsica that way. His whole mind seemed filled with Kenny Blacklaws. And it was taking him deeply into the past.

Quintin's own mother had died at his birth. His father had married a widow, Martha Blacklaws, when Quintin was seven. Her son, Kenny, had been four at the time. There had been a tacit antipathy between Kenny and Quintin from the beginning. And when Martha had died of pneumonia two years later, Kenny Blacklaws was just old enough to begin fighting Quintin. From that moment on, Garland could remember no moment of friendship or rapport, nothing but a maddeningly self-contained little devil tormenting him constantly. Blacklaws seemed a room closed and locked to the Garlands, something neither Quintin nor his father could ever see or reach or understand, with processes of mind so different from theirs he might have been born on another world. No amount of the beatings Martin Garland had given the boy mitigated that stubborn withdrawal.

And the mind. Garland could still remember watching that mind develop. Not particularly brilliant or versatile yet almost frightening in its methodical capacities for reading the meaning of all the little signs life left in its wake. Not a precocious talent that would attract great notice, but a faculty constantly, maddeningly brought to the notice of anyone closely associated with him.

Those earlier memories of Blacklaws faded before that last remembrance. It lay out there in the brush, where Bayou Lafitte backed up into a marsh, a few hundred yards south of the Garland home. It was night. Nine years ago. Quintin Garland was twenty years old. A twenty-year-old youth returning home from a day in the cotton fields his father hoped to turn into a fortune. An empty house. The bullwhip gone from its peg on the wall. It seemed Martin Garland was always down at the marsh with his stepson—and that whip.

After half an hour of waiting, Quintin went down there too. He found his father. There was no stepson and no whip. But there was his father, there was Martin Garland, lying half buried in the mud to one side of the trail, his head so beaten by a rock his face was unrecognizable. . . .

Garland snapped himself from the hateful reverie with effort, realizing how long he had stood at the window. He turned to get his cast-off Army greatcoat and shrugged into it, leaving the office. There was still a group loitering on the sagging steps of the two-story frame courthouse, across the street from the French House, when Garland came onto the street. He saw Roman's bald head and Gauche Sallier's black figure.

" 'Evening, counselor," laughed Roman. "Coming to the hanging?"

Garland thrust his hands deeply into the pockets of his coat and turned away to walk west on the street, bitter lines etching his face. There was no point in letting those fools goad him. The whole bunch of them wasn't worth a night's sleep. This whole town wasn't worth it. He had been a fool to come back. And yet—he could not help glancing over his shoulder—there would come a day, he would see the time when all of them were on their knees to him, little and big alike.

In this vitriolic mood he got his horse from the livery stable, a handsome Copperbottom, given to him by a client in lieu of cash. It was one of the few things of distinction left him, but he took no pleasure in its beauty as he trotted down Colonial Street, the main avenue that ran for a few blocks across the high plateau upon which the bulk of the town was situated and then dipped abruptly down into the hollow land behind the bluffs. The Mexican quarter was here, and he rode somberly between lines of squalid adobe hovels fronted by sagging spindle fences.

His home lay some ten miles west of Copper Bluffs, just off this wagon road, at the head of Bayou Lafitte. He was soon deeply submerged in the brushy land which constituted the eastern fringe of the Big Thicket. He trotted his horse through the tangle of thorny catclaw and mesquite, skirting potholes that rendered up a foul odor of stagnant water and rotten mud. He brushed irritably at Spanish moss that insisted on sweeping its clammy cerements against his face and cursed a looping grapevine that he failed to duck in time.

How could people love this land, the way Corsica and all the others seemed to? It was a hateful purgatory to him. He tried to shrug it away. He would be leaving soon enough. One way or another, he would get out. He wasn't going to waste his talents on a stupid, greasy-sack town like Copper Bluffs. One boost, just one step up, and he'd be on his way back to Austin, he'd take Corsica and. . . .

The Copperbottom spooked suddenly, almost unseating Garland as it jumped aside. With a curse he reined the animal back into the trail. But the horse shied again, trying to rear. He spun it around to bring the beast back down and saw what was the matter.

They came around a turn ahead, grunting deeply in their throats—a whole file of canebrake hogs, led by a spotted boar. It was low slung and razor backed, tusks gleaming like wicked scimitars from its bewhiskered lower jaw. At sight of the horse, the leader halted sharply, the others bunching up behind him, one upon the other, in a snorting pack, their tusks clashing against each other. Then the man appeared around the turn.

He was dressed in a ragged Mexican blanket, worn poncho style, with a hole in the center through which was thrust his head, leaving the four tails to dangle grotesquely about the hips of his rawhide leggins. These were so begrimed with a mixture of earth and clay and grease that they were almost black. He had a vacant, bucolic face, with a shallow jaw and suspicious little eyes that never remained focused long on one spot. He walked around the grunting hogs, tapping at their rumps with the rotten corncob he had been using to toll them with. His secretive grin caused his jaw to recede even more into a hairy neck.

" 'Evenin', Garland."

"I wish to hell you'd give some kind of warning, Tate," Garland swore, still fighting the fretting Copperbottom. "Isn't a horse in the county you haven't spooked with those razorbacks of yours."

Tate's bare feet had the prehensile length of a monkey's with black tufts of hair just behind the knobby joint of each toe. He curled these toes into the ooze, grinning in childish pleasure at the small chuckling sound this brought.

"Gotta git my hogs gathered in. King Wallace and his crowd are whipping up a hog hunt. Ain't going to render none of my piney-rooters up for lard." A childish transition of mood robbed his face of its vacant look, filling it with something vicious. "Think they kin take advantage of old Tate. Think they kin kill his hogs. He can't take their cows, kin he? Cut down one of Roman's longhorns, they'd kill him. Take one of Obermeier's hides, they'd hang him. But they kin have old Tate's hogs. Go right ahead and kill 'em. Those little piney-rooters are all he's got in the world, but it don't matter, jist go right ahead and kill 'em!" He spat suddenly and wiped the back of a grimy hand across his slack mouth. "Well, maybe old Tate kin do somethin'. They'll find out. Anybody take out after my hogs, it maybe won't be the hogs that git rendered up for lard . . . !''

Garland broke in impatiently. He had heard this tirade so often before. "You been south?"

Tate looked up in surprise, lips still parted. Then a cunning expression tucked in his eyes. He rolled his head back to leer up at Garland.

"It ain't down in Congo Bog, Garland."

"What isn't?"

"The hide factory where all these rustlers er taking the hides to be stripped off. It ain't down in Congo Bog."

"What makes you think I meant that?"

"I kin look inside a man, Garland. I kin read a man's heart. Lots of people like to know where that hidden packery is. But you'd like to know for different reasons than most." Tate frowned at him. "You're a lawyer-man, Garland. Wouldn't you have to turn the rustlers in if you found who they was?"

Garland stared down at the man, trying to read what lay in the vacuous face. Then he leaned confidingly toward Tate.

"Just suppose I didn't turn them in? Suppose I knew a way they could keep up their hide rustling, even on a larger scale, and never be touched by John Roman or any of the big operators?"

Tate chuckled. "Do you think the rustlers would let you in on it if you gave them something like that? Do you think it would make you lots of money, Garland?"

"I didn't say that."

"Neither did Kenny Blacklaws."

Garland bent sharply toward him. "Blacklaws?"

"Charlie Carew was at the line shack where Blacklaws is staying. Blacklaws met him there. I saw them from the Smoky Canes."

"Carew?" murmured Garland, righting himself in the saddle. He was staring off over Tate's head, with the implications of this running through him. "Why should Carew want to see Blacklaws?"

Tate grinned slyly. "Carew wants to know where the packery is, doesn't he?"

"But . . . Blacklaws?"

"Haven't you been wondering why Blacklaws come back?"

Garland did not answer the man, gripped by his own thoughts. The hogs had scattered off the trail now, rooting through the thickets. But one great sow, with a scaly hide tinted a strange luminous blue, had worked her way back to Tate and stood rubbing up against the man's leg like an affectionate cat. Tate tapped the corncob absently against her sharp back.

"Know what the lawyer-man's thinking, Teacup?" he asked the sow. "He's thinking it would be too bad if Kenny Blacklaws had been brought back by Carew. Blacklaws, now, he's a smart man. Out of all the men on the river he might be just the one to find that hidden hide factory. Wouldn't that be too bad? Then the lawyer-man'd never get a chance to tell the hide rustlers his scheme. Never get a chance to make himself a lot of money."

"Tate," said Garland softly, "Kenny used to go on those hog hunts with Mock Fannin when he was a kid. Did he ever kill one of your hogs?"

The sly humor was swept from Tate abruptly, and he was like a child with a tantrum. "If he did, he'd pay for it. Think they kin kill old Tate's hogs, they'll find out, think they kin kill my piney-rooters, it's them that'll git killed!"

"Is it, Tate?"

The hog toller broke off his vitriolic tirade. He stared up at Garland, a raging, pouting expression twisting his face. Slowly, then, this faded, and the slyness made indented pouches of his eyes, and he grinned blandly. "Why don't you just hire somebody to shoot Blacklaws, if you want him out of the way?"

"I didn't say I wanted him out of the way."

"Then what are you saying?"

"Have I ever killed one of your hogs, Tate?"

"Maybe."

Garland stiffened. "You know I've never been on a hog hunt in my life."

"Is that a fack?"

"What are you getting at?"

Tate cackled like an old woman. "Maybe someday you'll find out. Maybe someday you will."

Lips compressed, Garland frowned at him. Finally he said: "You never did say whether Blacklaws killed a hog of yours."

"You think that's my price, Garland?"

"Every man has one, they say."

The man glowered at the ground. "Not today."

"When?"

Tate bobbed the corncob against the blue sow's back again, staring vacantly into the timber. "Lawyer-man thinks Blacklaws is hunting the packery too now, Teacup. Afraid Blacklaws will find it before he can. But that ain't the only reason Garland wants Blacklaws out of the way, is it? You'n in me, we kin read men's hearts, can't we, Teacup? We kin look way down inside a man. Down to where it's been like a canker for nine years, like a big sore he can't heal. Down to where he's thought all this time Kenny Blacklaws killed his pa. Down to where he wants Blacklaws dead for it."

Chapter Four

Corsica Manatte dressed for dinner, though there was no occasion. It had been too long since she had done this or anything gay and frivolous and exciting. One of the few decent dresses she had left was the dark green moiré, draped at the hip, with enough décolleté to reveal the gleaming upper swell of her breasts. She worked her black hair into an upsweep, pinning it with the ivory comb her younger brother, Phil, had brought her from Houston, and put on her onyx earrings. The tarnished Adamesque mirror commanding her bedroom reflected a tall, handsome woman with a strikingly ripened body at breast and hip, light from the high candle sconces dropping strong shadows beneath the broad obliquity of her cheekbones to accent that faintly exotic cast of her face.

Somehow, though, this gave her none of the pleasure it should. *It was Quintin,* she decided, *and this afternoon. Why were they always quarreling lately?*

She got a cashmere shawl and swung it around her bare shoulders and went downstairs in this subdued mood. The only servant left to the Manattes was an immense Negress who had stayed on after the Emancipation, held by the ties and affections of the lifetime she had spent serving the family. Corsica looked in on Letty to make sure dinner was coming along all right and then moved restlessly out to the front gallery. From one shadowed end of this the monotonous creak of her father's cane rocker lapidated at her. Since the death of his wife, almost eight years ago, Troy Manatte had sunk into a pathetic senility, dwelling mostly in the past. He did not even seem to be aware that Corsica had come out.

She went on down the steps and walked out the *allée* which curved its way between untended cypresses to the river road. Her younger brother had not yet come back from Houston, and she was worried. Behind her the house rose bleakly into a tawny dusk. Time and neglect had allowed much of the outer plaster to fall from its walls, revealing the inner pattern of brick. The old French pantiles on the roof were crumbling, patched in many places by split cypress shingles, and the slender colonnettes supporting the gallery overhang had been left unpainted for so long they were turned almost black through weathering.

Yet, she realized, the family was lucky to possess it, even in this state. It was only at her mother's insistence that they had put some of their cotton money into Northern investments before the war. That war, and its following upheavals, had wiped out most of the big families. Those investments were all that allowed the Manattes to hang on now. The payments came quarterly, from the old family lawyer in Houston who still handled the stocks and bonds. Once in a while the money was late, and Phil would go to Houston to borrow against it.

Corsica reached the river road, with the vague murmur of the waters sighing up against her from the foot of the bluffs. She stood there a long time, trying to gain the refreshment this twilit land usually brought. Finally she caught sight of a rider coming around the turn in the river road. In this dusk he was featureless, and she voiced her natural assumption.

"Phil?"

There was a pause as he came on, and then he answered. "No, Corsica, it isn't Phil."

The rider's figure made a heavy-shouldered stain against the patina of the dying day. His face seemed to swim into focus, dusk filling its hollows with vague pools of shadow.

"Kenny," she said in a small voice.

He drew up a pace from her and sat with his long legs slacked against the leathers in that animal relaxation she remembered so well, his quiet smile lighting his face. " 'Evening, Corsica," he said.

"You've been back a long time," she murmured at last, "to make this your first visit."

"I didn't actually mean to drop in tonight," he said. "I've been pretty busy."

She sensed something withheld in him. It matched the reserve she felt in herself and put a barrier between them. As if he felt it too, the smile faded from his face. She had heard the talk after Blacklaws had fled the night of his stepfather's death. She had not wanted to believe it; yet now she knew a deep confusion at just what she felt toward him.

He was so much bigger and heavier than she remembered; his shoulders filled out the faded blue ducking jacket so massively. Every part of him seemed to emanate that immense, leashed strength. His hands lay one atop the other on the saddle horn. Their very quiescence was an expression of latent force, with the bluish pattern of cords curling down across the wrist and fanning out over rope-scarred ridges of muscle to meet the strong, blunt knuckles. Weather had colored his face darkly and etched a fine graining into the flesh, and the edges of his shaggy hair lay ink-black against the mahogany tint of it. In the poor light his eyes were inky as his hair, and she searched vainly for the kindling of little lights that could make them glow so warmly. The whole watchful somberness of his face almost frightened her. Then it fled, and that smile returned, bringing its boyishness to his face.

It brought Blacklaws back to her as she had known him before with a poignant rush, and it suddenly did not matter that she could not define most of her feelings toward him. She knew one. She knew she wanted his easy friendship once more with an eagerness she had not felt in years.

"We'd be glad to have you for dinner, Kenny. Dad's asked several times about you."

His smile broadened, his head tilted his acceptance, and he climbed off his horse to walk beside her back down the drive.

"You'll have so much to tell," she said. "It's like you've spent nine years in a foreign land."

"Not much to tell. Cattle in Wyoming. Stockyards in Kansas. Nothing but bread and beans at either. Even that gave out finally."

She realized he would give no more elaboration than this and was not surprised. He had shown this reticence even as a boy. Part of it was modesty, but a greater part was his deep self-sufficiency. A shrill voice broke against them from the dusk.

"That you, Phil?"

"No, Dad, it's Corsica. I found Kenny Blacklaws."

There was a sharp scraping sound, and then Troy Manatte's bent figure was crossing the lighted rectangles of French windows. He had once been as tall as Blacklaws, but now he was bent with age, most of his weight thrust against a Malacca cane. His white hair, backlighted by the windows, foamed off his head like a snowy nimbus. The myriad seams of his face were furry with senility, and his palsied hands were beginning to show the transparency of age. He swayed toward Blacklaws, squinting intensely.

"Martin let you come tonight, Kenny?"

Corsica did not miss the tightening reaction that ran across Blacklaws's face, and she said: "Dad, that was nine years ago."

His eyes fluttered to her, face blank for an instant. Then he frowned pathetically and shook his head.

"Nine years," he mumbled. "Seems like yesterday."

"Kenny's been up north," Corsica told the old man, not yet sure this was clear to him. "He just came back. You remember?"

"Yeah." Troy Manatte's fuzzy Adam's apple bobbed with his chuckle. "Well, a man's got to sow his wild oats, don't he, Kenny?"

Before Blacklaws could answer, there was the muffled sound of a horse coming up the outer drive. The darkness now was so thick that Corsica could just see the man as he swung in at a trot and dismounted before one of the ring posts. He must have seen Corsica's figure, silhouetted against the lighted glass doors, before he recognized who was with her.

"Corsica," Quintin Garland said. "I came to apologize for this afternoon."

He stopped then, close enough so that she could see his face. It was turned toward Blacklaws now. Corsica was suddenly swept with a sense of helplessness, as if she were outside all this, watching the people brought against each other, with nothing she could do or say having any control over it.

There was a faint clink of a French door opening, and the slouched figure of Corsica's older brother came through the portal. He peered down past the three of them, standing at the head of the steps.

"Well, Quintin," he said in his ironic voice, "staying to supper?"

Corsica could not help her sharp wheeling motion to-

41

ward Dee Manatte, anger flattening the curve of her cheek. Had he done that deliberately?

But it was too late now, for already her father was saying: "Yes, Quintin, light and sup. Kenny's here too. Did you see him? I'll send old Josh for your dad, and we'll have a regular banquet."

Under any other circumstances, Corsica realized, Garland would have declined the invitation, if it would save causing her embarrassment. But what lay between these two men seemed to pit them together on a plane that transcended their ordinary lives.

"Thank you, Mister Manatte," Garland said. "I'd be glad to stay."

"Good, good." Troy Manatte pounded his cane on the floor. "And afterwards we'll all take a ride. I've got a new stud I'd like to show you. I'll go get my ridin' gear on right now."

The old man wheeled, almost upsetting himself, and hobbled through the open front door. A malicious relish of the scene was in Dee's dry voice.

"It's a pity such old friends have to stand out here waiting for the fence worm to rot. Why can't we all come inside?"

Blacklaws was the first to turn. Corsica watched Garland with a silent plea in her eyes, but he did not seem to be aware of that. His attention was so taken up with Blacklaws that he even forgot his manners and came up the steps to go through the door before Corsica. She followed them helplessly, a little surprised to see that Garland was as tall as Blacklaws. She had thought of Kenny as bigger, somehow. Perhaps it was that Garland did not have Blacklaws's massive upper frame. He was narrower through the shoulders and hips, yet it was a hard narrowness that robbed him of no strength. It merely seemed a strength directed differently from Blacklaws's, formed of nervous movement and eager vitality, like a hound straining at the leash. It was something she had always admired about him, in a country where apathy had descended upon so many people.

Dee had already stepped back in through the French doors and was pouring drinks from a cut-glass decanter on the butternut sideboard. He was a tall boy, in his middle twenties, something prematurely aged about his gaunt face. He had inherited the black hair of the Manattes, letting it go shaggy to mat up over his ears and down the back of his neck.

"A toast to Kenny's return," he chuckled.

"How nice of you to play the host, Dee," Corsica said thinly.

His face turned up toward her. An eager light filled his tilted eyes, like a puppy waiting for a game to start. He handed the drinks around, lifted his.

"To Kenny's return," he said.

Garland got his glass half way to his compressed lips then lowered it. Blacklaws let his back down without drinking.

"You don't welcome it," he said.

"Did you think I would?" asked Garland.

A faint strain seemed to fill Blacklaws's cheeks. Corsica knew a painful desire to turn the course of this.

"Kenny was in Wyoming," she said. She was startled at the brittleness of her voice.

"Quintin went away, too, you know," Dee told Blacklaws. "Law school in Austin. Even got a job in the attorney general's office. Why didn't you stay, Quintin?"

"Dee," Corsica said sharply, "you know why he came back."

"Yeah?" Dee grinned. Garland was holding the stem of his glass so tightly it splayed and whitened the ends of his fingers. Dee shrugged at Blacklaws. "Have to admire his courage, anyway, Kenny. Putting up such a gallant fight for the little operators. Roman and Obermeier have had six separate men up on one charge or another during the last three months. Garland's defended every one of them.'' He shook his head sadly. ''I just can't believe they were all guilty.''

''Dee!'' Corsica's voice escaped her angrily.

Garland turned to face the fireplace, his back turned toward them. ''Never mind, Corsica,'' he said tightly. ''We all know your brother's quaint sense of humor.''

There was an awkward pause. Blacklaws took a drink then turned to sit down in the shabby lyre-arm sofa. At this moment the clatter of boots came from the hall outside. Dee wheeled with that graceful swiftness he was so capable of on rare occasions, walking to the door. He reached the opening just as Phil Manatte came into view in the hall. Phil was the younger brother, just twenty, as tall as Dee without the weight of a man's form filling out his chest and shoulders. There was a harried expression in his blue eyes as he tried to brush past Dee, hanging onto his right arm with his other hand. His batwing chaps and heavy hip-length mackinaw were covered with a whitish grime that crumbled off his boots to dribble across the hall floor with every step.

''Phil,'' said Dee, catching at him. ''What is it?''

''Leave me go,'' said the younger boy, tearing free and turning to climb the stairway. Anger pinched at Dee's face, and he followed the boy up. He caught him out of sight, near the top, and Corsica could hear their angry voices. She sent a helpless look at the two men remaining in the parlor.

''If you want to go, Corsica,'' said Blacklaws, ''everything will be all right here, I promise you.''

''Thanks, Kenny,'' she said and rose to walk from the room to the stairs. Dee had Phil backed up against the rail near the top.

''You didn't go to Houston. That's shell mud on your

boots. Now tell me where you've been, Phil . . . ?''

"Dee," cried Corsica, "let the boy alone."

Dee whirled on her, anger robbing his face of its sardonic humor. "I'm tired of all this mystery, Corsica."

"You're being terrible tonight," she said. "Baiting Blacklaws and Garland down there . . . and now this."

Dee slackened against the banister, mockery rising up in a defensive veil across his eyes. "Well, now, little gal's older brother didn't make his sis mad with his innocent little pleasures, did he?"

"Innocent?" she asked. "You know how little it took to set Quintin and Kenny at each other when they were kids. You know what liquor does to Quintin. So you fill him up with that atrocious peach brandy and prod him about the trials till he's ready to fly apart anyway. . . ." She broke off, realizing her voice was loud enough to carry downstairs. She lowered it to an intense tone. "You go downstairs and bring Dad from his room, Dee. Take him to the dining room and get him seated. And I swear, if I find you back in that living room before I come down, I'll . . . I'll . . . !"

"You'll what, darlin'?"

"You force me to say it," she told him. "I'll cut off your allowance."

His cheeks seemed to draw in, filling his face with gaunt surprise. Then he lifted away from the banister, anger making his eyes glow. "You wouldn't dare."

"Just go on baiting those two and find out," she said.

He continued to stare at her, lips parted faintly. Then, without a word, he cut around her and went downstairs at a hard walk. She faced about to Phil, who still stood against the banister.

"What happened, Phil?"

"Horse took a tumble. Just let me change clothes, will you? I'm splattering mud all over your house."

"Everything's all right?"

"If you mean the money, I got it."

She watched him turn and go to his room. The sound from downstairs brought her about then. Garland was speaking, voice strained and tight.

"You must have known there weren't any more jobs to be had down here than there were up in Wyoming. Why did you come back?"

There was a treacherous silence, and Corsica hurried downstairs. She reached the living room to find Garland standing with his back to the fireplace, the decanter in one hand, a full glass in the other. His face was flushed, his eyes glittering brightly, and she realized he must have been drinking steadily. Blacklaws sat on the sofa, the weight of him depressing the pillows deeply. The utter lack of humor in his face gave him that older look. His eyes were half lidded and withdrawn, watching Garland steadily. She could almost see his mind at work, judging each little sign in Garland, deciding where it was leading.

Before she could speak, the tinkle of spur chains came from the hall behind her. Troy Manatte came from his bedroom with ancient batwing chaps flapping at skinny legs and a pair of Navy revolvers holstered at his waist, their weight throwing him off balance at every step.

"Tell the boys I'm ready," he said, hardly looking at her as he went on by. He flung open the front door and stomped out, halting at the top step to stand there peering out into the night. Dee came down the hall from the rear, shrugging at Corsica.

"I couldn't do nothing with him. He was bent on riding tonight. That black stud's been dead ten years, and he still thinks he's goin' to top it."

Now the old man had half turned, a puzzled frown on his face. He passed a hand across his forehead in a helpless gesture. Then he walked down to the end of the gallery. His chair complained raucously as he lowered himself into it. That steady squeak of cane began once more, as he started rocking.

"You still haven't told me why you came back," Garland told Blacklaws, pouring himself another drink.

Corsica turned impatiently into the room. "What does it matter? A man can have his own reasons for coming back to his home."

Garland's eyes flashed wickedly in the light. "The same reasons that made him go away?"

Blacklaws rose so swiftly from the couch that Corsica's breath stopped. But he only turned and moved around the lyre arms to the French windows, a solid shape against their checkering of small panes, and then stood, looking out.

"Why *did* you go away, Kenny?" asked Dee. "There was a lot of talk about it. Right on the same day Martin was killed with his head all bashed in that way."

"Yes," Garland said. "With his head all bashed in that way."

"Please," protested Corsica. "This can't help."

"Perhaps it can," Blacklaws murmured. "You mentioned talk, Dee. What kind of talk?"

Dee shrugged, watching Garland's face, a sly appreciation of this lighting his eyes. "You know what goes around about something like that."

"Can't say that I do," Blacklaws told him.

"I'll tell you, then," Garland said. An unnatural flush filled his face. "They said you killed my father."

Corsica could see the muscles bunch up across Blacklaws's shoulders. For a while she thought he did not mean to turn or even answer. Finally Blacklaws came about to face Garland. The clenched muscles in his jaw made it look heavier. His eyes were so hooded by the lids they were barely visible.

"And what do you think?" he asked softly.

Garland was the lawyer now, relishing the pause he

brought to this, with the attention of the whole room on him.

"I think Dad had taken you out into the bayou to thrash you," he said then. "You turned on him, and you murdered him."

For just that instant Corsica saw Blacklaws's reaction. It was like a wash of brackish water flooding against his face and ebbing away to leave it darkened and muddy. Then she could almost see him deliberately draining himself of its violence. It seemed a painfully long time before he spoke.

"It helps a man to know exactly where he stands," he said at last. "But I promised Corsica everything would be all right. You can't get anything out of me in this house."

Garland's response must have been completely thoughtless, brought on by the release of drink and his own wild frustration at being unable to goad Blacklaws. Corsica saw it welling up in his eyes.

"Quintin . . . !"

As if her voice had set it off, he flung glass and all at Blacklaws's face. It struck Blacklaws on the cheek, the amber liquor splashing across his whole face. The tumbler dropped unbroken to the floor. Blacklaws's eyes flew open an instant after they had closed. His whole body came forward onto the balls of his feet. She saw Garland spread his boots to meet it, a triumph in his parted lips.

Then Blacklaws was settling back, his eyes closing till they had the squinted look of a whipped man. Carefully he reached up to wipe the liquor off his face with the back of a hand. It was dripping from his jaw to form an ever-widening stain on his shirt. His voice trembled faintly when he finally spoke.

"I told you, you can't bring me to a fight in this house, Quintin."

Garland remained there a moment longer, face white and wild. Then he wheeled and walked viciously past Corsica. She saw the blank look in his eyes and realized he did not even see her. The three of them stood in a static silence till the door slammed, and the porch trembled beneath Garland's feet, running now.

" 'Evenin', Quintin," called Troy Manatte. "Give your dad my regards."

Corsica's eyes were on Blacklaws now. He was standing with both fists closed tightly. His eyes seemed fixed on the far wall. She moved to him, catching his arm. She was shocked at the tension filling his body.

"I'm sorry, Kenny," she said.

His voice trembled. "Are you?"

She frowned at him and then realized what must be in his mind. "You think I knew Garland was coming too?"

"Didn't you?"

"Kenny. . . ." She broke off, backing away from him. "I refuse to dignify that with an answer," she said.

He turned to look at her. Finally he spoke stiffly. "I think I'd better go too, Corsica."

She watched him till he was out the door. She was suddenly afraid that he would meet Quintin outside and hurried to the French doors. But from there she saw that Quintin's Copperbottom was gone from the ring posts. Blacklaws unhitched Tar Baby and swung aboard with that economy of effort, turning the black mare out into the darkness. Dee chuckled softly from behind.

"Well, look at all the fireworks."

Tension left Corsica in a tide. She was abruptly too drained to feel anger at her brother. She went upstairs to her room and sat down on the tester bed in the dark. She wanted to cry and couldn't, wanted to meet this with some adequate emotion and couldn't. Finally, she turned up the oil lamp and went to her closet. She moved out a wicker hamper to reach down behind and lift out the whip. She took this back to the bed and sat down and stared at it a long time, trying to resolve it all in her mind.

It was an old blacksnake about ten feet long, a whip she had found hidden in her father's room two years ago. She had never been able to make him tell where he had gotten it. On the stock carved into the wood was a name. *Martin Garland.*

Chapter Five

Kenny Blacklaws awoke to a foggy dawn in the old, abandoned line shack by Smoky Canes. He rolled out of his worn blankets and groggily pulled on his clothes. Figments of the night before kept coming to him. He had half expected Garland to be waiting in the grove around the Manatte house or along the river, but apparently the man's anger had left him no patience for that.

Thought of Garland's anger made Blacklaws think of his own. He felt a vague sickness as he recalled how it had gripped him last night. It was something he had feared all the way down from Laramie. It was something that had haunted him all those nine years he had been away. It was why he had practiced control so assiduously, why he had deliberately tried to drain himself of emotion through all that time, so it could not betray him again. And for what?

Roman hadn't been able to make him mad. That

showed something. Even Charlie Carew and that dirty
swindle the man had pulled to get him back hadn't really
made him mad. That showed he had gained some control
through those years. But not enough. That was the insidious fear that had lain beneath his long struggle.
Enough for Roman or Charlie Carew or other men. But
not enough for Quintin Garland. Why should that be?
Were its roots in the deep antipathy that had lain between Quintin and Blacklaws from the first, seeming to
fate them to antagonism on whatever level they met? Or
did it go farther than that? Was it because Quintin was
Martin Garland's son and so inextricably involved with
all that had happened?

It was taking Blacklaws back now. Nine years back.
Down in the black mud of Bayou Lafitte where a
shaggy-headed boy stood spread-legged on that little
patch of solid ground, shaken by a rage and reaction he
could no longer control. *You won't touch me with that
whip again, Martin, I swear it. I didn't run that horse
through your cotton today, and you're not going to whip
me for it . . . !*

Blacklaws closed his eyes, trying to blot out the memory. It had not come to him so vividly in years. But he
could not lose the ugly picture of it, the one time when
he had lost himself completely to emotion and had ruined his whole life by it. He had sworn his passions
would never rule him again. And yet he could not prevent recalling the helplessness he had felt before the anger Quintin had drawn from him last night. If the man
had just prodded him once more. . . .

Blacklaws rose from the bunk, trying to shake it from
his mind. He made a fire in the stove then got a can of
hog lard and fingered into his frying pan what little remained. Putting this over the flames to melt, he un-
wrapped the rest of the catfish he had caught the day
before, rolled the strips of white meat in corn meal, and

dropped them into the pan. He forced his mind to consider the other things that had happened last night, piecing them together, adding one thing onto the next like a man piling bricks into a wall.

Phil was supposed to have been in Houston? That white grime on his pants didn't come from the Houston road, Blacklaws thought. *Only place you get marked like that is down around the shell islands. What would he be doing there? Rustling? Why? Phil was always the more decent of those two boys. Not the type to turn bad just because of a little hard times. He'd need a bigger reason than that. I wonder if the Manatte stocks are really paying off. This drop in the beef market has begun to hit the North too. Say the stocks weren't paying. That would be a big enough reason. Not for his own selfish interests. For Corsica and the family. That sounds more like Phil.*

That brought him to Corsica. *Had she looked like she was trying to hide something when Phil came in? No. More surprised and puzzled. But maybe she was a good actress*. Blacklaws was reluctant to consider it in that light, but he had to look at all the possibilities. His very reluctance was dangerous. *Because a woman could draw emotion from him too. A different kind of emotion than Garland brought and yet just as dangerous, if emotion was a man's weakness, and the woman was in a position to use it against him. Was Corsica in that position?* He shook his head vaguely, continually presented with the image of the woman herself rather than her motives. *How poignantly the beauty of her had struck him. There had been other women in these last nine years, but none of them struck at his most jealously guarded sources the way the mere presence of Corsica could. Perhaps part of this was the fact that she knew him so well. But the other part was her beauty, her ripened, yearning womanhood that seemed to melt all a man's defenses.*

The nervous shiftings of his horse in the corral broke

in on Blacklaws's thoughts. He listened a moment, then his caution took hold. He slid the frying fish off the fire and got his Remington from its holster, where it hung from the cartridge belt on a wall peg. He scooped up the empty water bucket and put his gun in it. Then he opened the door, surveying the park before he stepped out. It was still empty. He walked unhurriedly out and down the wall to the corner of the house. Once around on the blind side, he flattened up against the wall and pulled his gun from the bucket. This side was faced toward the canebrake, so dense a man could not move within them unless he set up a rattling. Blacklaws was hidden from any other direction of approach.

The movements of Tar Baby now became more marked, as she snorted and pawed and ran up and down a side of the pole corral. Finally she threw up her ugly hammer head and gave a shrill whinny. There was an answering neigh from the open over toward the pine grove. Then the drawling voice.

"Now, Myrtle, you don't want to make so much noise. You know how smart that Blacklaws yak is. He might have stepped around the corner of that shack real innocent-like, making everybody think he was only going after water, when really he had his cutter dumped in that bucket and is just waiting there now to shoot the beans out of you."

Blacklaws felt the tension slip from him. His smile broadened the lower part of his face, lending it that youth, as he stepped around the corner of the shack to see the rider.

"Man flogs his life out beating the brush for scalawags," Blacklaws said, "and then one rides right up to his house."

Mock Fannin drew rein on his little bay pony, slickened by the dampness of the fog till its hide looked red as wet blood. Cousin of the Manattes, son of an Irish cattle agent who had married Troy Manatte's sister, Mock himself was probably the most disreputable man in a land of disreputable men without giving any actual cause for such a reputation other than a congenital distaste for work, washing, and the truth.

He bore none of the Manatte refinements. He was a short and burly man with a sloppy belly that rolled out in grimy folds over the beltless waistband of filthy rawhide leggins which were mottled clownishly with varicolored patches of hide and linsey-woolsey. He was not much past thirty, but jowls had already formed about his mouth, and the deep creases made by these meaty bulges gave his face a leathery look above his scrubby growth of black beard.

"Dropped over Manatte way last night just after you left," he grinned. "Corsica told me you lit a shuck so fast they didn't get a chance to invite you to the hog hunt today." He paused, the grin fading. "You tangled with a poison pup there, Kenny."

"Garland?" Blacklaws shrugged. "Nothing much I can do about it, Mock."

"You can keep right on being as watchful as you was this morning," Mock said.

Blacklaws looked up to see the grin again, sly and knowing, creasing Mock's unshaven face. He could not help answering it, and in a moment both of them were chuckling deeply with the easy comradeship they had known so many years before.

"I'll get my gear," Blacklaws said. "Where are they gathering?"

"Gumbo Meadows," Mock told him. "Rouquette's place."

Blacklaws saddled up and led Tar Baby from the corral and got a couple of bullhide buckets for the lard, tying them back of the cantle. Then he swung aboard and lined out southward with Mock at his hip. The sun was beginning to come through the haze now, bringing a pale, diffused light that caused both men to squint. Its heat lifted sour odors of rotten mud from the bayous, and now and then from the west came the dank redolence of a freshly plowed field.

They passed casual conversation for a while, and then Mock asked: "What are you doing with the hides, Kenny?"

It took Blacklaws a little by surprise. "King Wallace goes to Galveston every now and then. Hauls a wagon load for me for a quarter of the sale."

"Wouldn't you rather have the full amount?"

"Haven't got a wagon myself."

Mock sent him a sidelong glance. "I'm insulted you'd play dumb with me."

Blacklaws felt tension curling up within him. "I suppose you've got a hide factory hidden out in the grove."

"What if I had, Kenny, would you work with me?"

Blacklaws could not help turning to the man now and frowning. "You?"

"Why not?" chuckled Mock. "I've got a setup down south of Bayou Lafitte that'll strip a thousand hides a day and render a hundred tons of lard. I got markets in Galveston, Tampa, New Orleans, almost any place you want to mention."

Blacklaws free-bitted his mare through flags ringing a pothole, frowning at the animal's twitching ears. There was a tingling excitement in him. He couldn't believe this.

"You can't do all that alone," he said.

"John Roman's with me," Mock said casually.

This time Blacklaws could not hide his surprise. "Roman?"

Mock's giggle was sly. "You wouldn't've thought it, would you? What better setup could we have? Nobody'd suspect a big operator like him. If anybody'd figure it out, you would. And you didn't. That proves it's good. The way Roman runs around the country kicking every little operator he can find and screaming how much of his beef they're rustling.''

"And who else?" asked Blacklaws carefully.

Mock turned to squint at him. "Seems to me you're mighty curious."

"You already told me enough to hang you."

Mock's chuckle shook his sloppy belly. "All right. Just shows how much I trust you."

"Phil Manatte?"

Mock shrugged. "He works for me off and on. Too young to trust much."

"And maybe Quintin's in on the deal?"

Mock looked sharply at him then pursed his lips and shook his head. "Too unreliable. We don't need any legal advice anyway. We're doing right pretty without it."

"How pretty?"

"Hundred thousand dollars a year."

A network of cow-track wrinkles spread away from Blacklaws's squinting eyes with the grin creeping across his face. "You old scalawag," he said. Then he threw back his head and let out the first hearty laugh he had given in months. "You damned old scalawag," he shouted. "You almost got the drop on me. I've been away so long I forgot what a real liar sounded like. John Roman and Phil Manatte and a thousand hides a day. If you hadn't thrown in that hundred thousand dollars a year, you'd have had me. I haven't heard anything to top that in nine years. I've heard some powerful liars up north, but they sound like preachers beside you."

Mock looked at him with a hurt expression. "You don't believe me?"

"Sure I believe you," said Blacklaws, still laughing.

"Let's go out and skin a few thousand steers this morning."

Mock sighed. "Nobody ever believes me. Here I offer you the best thing you'll get in a lifetime, and you think I'm prevaricating."

They rode on, and Blacklaws felt good, really good, for the first time since his return. Then that faded, and he knew it was the letdown. He could not help feeling it. For a moment there he had thought this was it. He should have known it would never come that easy—an old friend walking up and handing him the whole thing on a silver platter. He should be glad it wasn't true. He wouldn't want Mock mixed up in it.

"What made you think Garland was working for me?" Mock asked him.

"I saw Tate out in the canes day before yesterday," Blacklaws told him. "He asked me how I thought it could be fixed so hides could be rustled and Roman and Obermeier wouldn't be able to do anything about it. Somehow I couldn't see such an idea originating with Tate. It sounded more like a legal twist."

Mock emitted a disgusted snort. "Tate's already passed that word along. Sure it wasn't his idea. It comes from Garland. He has something on Roman, I guess. Thinks it might be worth a lot to the rustlers."

"I knew Garland had bad streaks in him. I never really thought he'd get on the wrong side of the trail."

"Why do you suppose he came back?" said Mock. "Not because he thought the little men needed him back here. Didn't you hear about the attorney general being kicked out for taking a bribe?"

"The attor . . . ?" Blacklaws looked at him impatiently. "You mean Garland took a bribe down in Austin?"

"No. The attorney general."

"Is he disbarred?"

"The attorney general?"

"No. Garland. Come out of the woods, Mock. If Garland was caught taking a bribe, he'd be disbarred."

"Maybe they didn't have enough proof for that. Maybe it just put such a stain on his name that he couldn't make out in any of the bigger cities and had to come back here. Maybe I'm the only one around here who knows about it. I was in Austin at the time. It was a hushed-up affair."

"And now he's up against the wall even here," mused Blacklaws. "Roman and the others have ruined it for him. This rustling is just about the last chance he'll have."

"He's still got that ambition eating at him, Kenny. The same thing that ruined his father. It's the biggest thing in his life. It always has been. You know that as well as I do. He'd give his soul to sit the top saddle in this county."

"Do you think he means to expose the rustlers if they fall for his offer and make contact?"

Mock shook his head. "More like him to demand a cut. There's big money in it, Kenny. Hundred thousand dollars a year."

Blacklaws rode on without answering. He found himself starting that old habit of mind, putting this fact against all the others, shifting them back and forth against each other till he found the right fit. Then he checked himself. Mock knew him too well. It would be a mistake to let the man see how much this meant to him.

Chapter Six

They passed through a string of cypress swamps on a spongy trail before they finally reached Gumbo Meadows, a stretch of salt-grass prairies strung out through the chinquapins and loblolly pines a few miles west of the Sabine. At the edge of one of these meadows Rouquette had his shack, a squalid log structure set up on brick piers to escape the annual floods in this low country. There was already a crowd of horses and men and dogs about the cabin when Blacklaws and Mock came into the meadow.

Blacklaws saw both Phil and Dee Manatte squatted down with their backs against the piers, talking with Rouquette. He was an immense man, well over six feet, the muscles laced across his body like bulging snakes. His mixture of Choctaw Indian and Santo Domingan Negro was called Os Rouge in Louisiana. It gave him a skin that glistened like oiled mahogany in the sun, the red tints glowing to life momentarily whenever his movement caused the light to catch them up.

Over by the steps was the cotton farmer, King Wallace, and his son, Gabe. They both had their barlow knives out and were whittling at soft cedar sticks while they talked with Hush Collins, a bowlegged little brush-popper in his sixties, who ran a small cut of cows over in the westerly fringes of the Big Thicket. He claimed it was a Caddo arrow through his throat that had left him unable to speak above a hoarse whisper. At sight of Blacklaws, Dee Manatte unfolded onto his feet, that loose grin lifting his lips.

"Well, if it ain't the catamount of Copper Bluffs, still alive and kicking. I thought Garland was all set to jump you in the brush last night."

Blacklaws shrugged, reining his horse in. "Didn't show his light."

"You should have jumped down his craw at the house," Dee told him.

Blacklaws met his gaze squarely, a half-lidded demand in his eyes. "Disappointed?" he asked.

Dee shifted indolently away from the wall, still smiling. "You ain't afraid of Garland, are you, Kenny?"

"You always got to prod your way through a thicket?" asked Phil Manatte irritably. "Can't you just sit back and relax sometimes?"

"Talk about thickets," Mock told Phil, "I hear you was down my way last night. Why didn't you drop by?"

A startled look caught at Phil's youthful face. He blanketed that off deliberately. "I wasn't down your way, Mock," he said. "What gave you that idea?"

"Well, now, I don't know," said Mock, "except there was about four hundred skinned carcasses stinking up the bayou in front of my place when I woke up this morning. I knew nobody except you could do all that in one night, without help."

A nervous laugh shook Phil's body. "Damn you," he said. "Sure it wasn't four thousand?"

Rouquette's bone-white teeth flashed in a wide grin. "Sure, sure," he said. "Four thousand. And they all had wing and fin on them. How about we step on our hay burners and hunt up these hogs before Mock here has us believe they turned into carpetbaggers and are goin' to take over Jefferson County."

He turned to go around behind the shack after his

corralled horse, but Blacklaws did not miss the momentary settling of his glance on Phil Manatte. The Os Rouge came back in a few minutes in the saddle, and the rest of them took to their animals, a half dozen hound dogs lifting themselves out of shady spots, gathering in an eager bunch before the riders. Recent rain had brought an early bloom of bluebonnets, filling the open patches with their white-tipped growth, like so many rabbits waving their cottontails to the sun.

The cavalcade soon left the open prairies and plunged into the twilit paths of the bayous, passing under gnarled cypresses with mustang vines looping down off their branches, as big around as a man's arm. Here and there a post oak flung the long shadows of its waxy green leaves in a casual dappling across a sunny patch. Steam lay in serpentine shreds through the woods, sucked from the land by the heat, carrying with it the putrefying stench of the ancient earth.

Mock and Blacklaws had ridden southwest from the line cabin to reach Gumbo Meadows, and now they were continuing their direction, until the upper margins of Congo Bog came into view. This was a vast, little-known swampland bordered on the west by the Neches and on the east by the Sabine, running south for ten miles to Lake Sabine and the coast. It had gotten its name in the early part of the century when a band of fleeing slaves had sought refuge in its fastness and had never been heard of again. Since then the rumors and legends of mysterious disappearances and deaths had grown with the years. There were tales of quicksand that would suck a man down in a second, giant cottonmouths remaining from a bygone age, and endless reaches of bog across which there were no trails. Blacklaws himself had penetrated its fringes once or twice, hunting with Phil, but they had not gone in far. He knew of no white man who had gone very deep and returned to tell of it, though he had always suspected Mock of knowing more about its interior than anyone else.

"Now I hear from Deller you've moved away from Mexican Creek and set up shop in the bog," Blacklaws told him.

"Too crowded on Mexican Creek," Mock told him. "Anybody gets in a day's ride of me I feel cramped."

"How deep in the bog are you?"

"Seventeen miles."

"Find any of those big cottonmouths?"

"Every morning on my doorstep. Seventeen feet long. I have plenty of dead bodies to feed them, and they leave me alone."

The land broke up into fingers of water lying green and stagnant between stretches of wind-tossed reed beds and clumps of dashing cane. The first hog broke out of his hiding in the reeds almost underfoot, charging off through a shallow lagoon with a great splashing and roaring. More of them burst from the reed beds to run before the men, but the riders ignored this until they had reached the largest patch of reeds and canes in the marsh. Here they halted, dumping their lard pails and rendering equipment at the base of a cypress.

"I been scout these lagoons all this winter," Rouquette told them. "They's enough piney-rooters fatten up on the acorn in there to feed all of Jefferson County. Ken, you and the Manatte stay here with the great liar. The rest of us we ride on around the other side. Give us chance to reach our place, then light up."

Mock watched the Os Rouge and Hush and the Wallaces ride out across a lagoon, splashing knee deep through the water and then turned to the remaining men. "Who's got a match?"

Phil produced some and got off his horse, picking his way carefully through the reeds, feeling with each step for sure ground till he reached the main bed. Here he hunted a long time for dry fuel for kindling, piling it up in a couple of spots. Then he ignited this. The rain-dampened reeds responded sullenly, sending up a black smoke. Red flames began to flicker through the smoke, lapping at the base of post oaks and cypresses whose roots and trunks were so saturated with water they refused to burn. Here and there a tongue of outlying grass ignited, and formed a cackling little line of fire.

Then the flags within the reed bed began to flame. A chorus of grunts and snorts arose, and the first wild hog erupted heavily from the reeds with a crash, squealing as a tongue of fire singed its neck. It was a long-snouted, young shoat, rolling in tallow from its recent diet of acorns, sharp hoofs churning up mud as it ran.

"There goes taller," shouted Mock. "First one's mine."

He wheeled toward the shoat, firing. The pig stumbled, dug its snout in the mud, and with a wild squeal tried to spin away. Mock ran his red pony after it, slopping fetlock deep into the rotten mud, firing the second time.

Blacklaws lost him then as half a dozen more burst from the burning reeds and scattered toward them. He picked a fat sow and fired three times before she went down.

"They're coming now," Dee yelled across to Rouquette. "Watch for them old granddaddies. They're the worst."

The muffled explosion of shots rose from the opposite side of the reed bed. Blacklaws's sow was down, sinking heavily into the mud. He wheeled Tar Baby away from the sidelong lunge of a young boar, as it tried to hook him with one of its gleaming tusks, while it ran by. He spun in the saddle, throwing down to shoot as it ran away from him on his other side. But at the same moment Dee came into his vision, already firing. The hog

63

jerked in mid-stride and went rolling over and over, feet kicking.

Phil was racing over to the south tip of the reed bed, yelling that a whole herd of them was coming out of the thickets there. Dee whirled his animal on a hind heel to follow his younger brother. At the same time Mock shouted from behind Blacklaws.

"Turn it around, Kenny, here comes the first-old grandpa!"

A keen apprehension ran through Blacklaws, causing him to put his off-rein hard against Tar Baby's neck, spinning the mare back toward the reed bed. These old boars had remained within the bed until it had almost burned over and now, when they could no longer stand the heat, they were coming out, singed and maddened. They were bigger than the sows and the shoats, mottled hides scarred by the brush and by many battles, their curved tusks gleaming wickedly as they ran, snorting, into the open. One was breaking to run between Mock and Blacklaws. Mock wheeled his animal to cut off the hog. But Blacklaws's mare was a good chopping horse, and she had already veered to cut across the boar's line of direction without any signals from her rider.

Blacklaws opened fire at the hog. It took the rest of his bullets to stop it. Even then he had to spin away in the last instant, as the boar lunged past, going down. Another pair of boars had burst from the reeds, and Mock turned his grunting bay to tail them. He split them up, and one turned toward the post oaks north of the reed bed. Yelling wildly, Mock plunged after this boar, opening fire. The hog disappeared into the dark shadows beneath the trees.

"Don't go in there after him, Mock," yelled Blacklaws. "He'll get your horse where it can't run."

But Mock's own yelling kept him from hearing Blacklaws, and his excitement blocked off all caution.

The second boar had cut around behind Mock's horse, but Blacklaws's oncoming mare caused it to turn again in the same direction that Mock was running. Blacklaws hauled up, hoping the hog would not follow Mock once the pressure was off. The squealing boar did not see this and plunged into the trees right behind Mock.

Blacklaws put the spurs to Tar Baby in a genuine fear for Mock, pinched in as he was between those two. He went into the trees at a dead run, mud slopping up head high from his animal's churning hoofs. Then they hit grassed-over ground that made a squeaking sound beneath the running animal. The brush thickened, with palmettos rearing up in a waist-high mass of tossing fronds to whip at Tar Baby. Blacklaws reined her left to dance through a pair of post oaks grown three feet apart. Their waxen leaves splattered across Blacklaws's face, blinding him. He heard the smash of heavy brush beneath him, felt it claw at his leggins, opened stinging eyes just in time to duck beneath a low-swinging grapevine. Then he heard a stertorous grunting ahead, accompanied by the clatter of broken brush and erupted into an open glade, right on the tail of that hog behind Mock.

The scene played itself out in that last instant, while he was still plunging in on it. Mock was racing at the thick wall of canes and brush at the other side of this glade. Apparently the hog he was chasing had already plunged into the thicket and, finding it impenetrable farther in, he had whirled to come back. Just as Mock's horse reached the fringe of brush, the spotted boar came charging out. Mock fired point-blank, going right on in over the hog.

It jerked with the impact of the bullet but plunged in between the bay's legs before going down, tossing its head up in a last spasm to gore the horse. The tusk ripped the bay's belly front to rear, as it ran on over the hog. The horse leaped into the air with a wild scream, pitching Mock off, and then went down kicking into the tangle of brush, blood spouting over Mock as he hit. He rolled to his hands and knees, mottled with blood and mucky earth, crouching there in a daze.

The hog was down too, in the middle of the glade, grunting its life out with Mock's bullet in its body. The boar ahead of Blacklaws immediately turned toward its companion, running over there to protect the dying hog, as was their habit, wheeling with its rump in toward the fallen animal, head jerking up and down in ugly little movements. Blacklaws turned his horse toward Mock, throwing down on the remaining hog. There was a metallic click, and he remembered he had fired his last shot. He had reached Mock by then, and he reined his mare in, trying to reload. But Tar Baby was so spooked by the smell of blood and the fear of that grunting boar that she fought his reins, fiddling and rearing.

"Climb aboard before that rooter charges," Blacklaws shouted at Mock. "I can't let go this horse to reload."

Mock pawed hazily at the mare to help him rise, sending her to kicking wildly. Blacklaws was almost pitched off before he fought the animal down and swung her around so that Mock's pawing hands caught a stirrup leather instead of a hind leg. Then Blacklaws held the fretting beast there while Mock climbed erect, pulling heavily on the leather.

"Get on!" said Blacklaws. "Grandpa catches you down there we'll have your guts looped on that post oak!"

"That tumble clabbered my brains," Mock told him, reeling heavily into the bronc as he tried to climb aboard. "Where in hell are you, Ken . . . ?"

He broke off, and Blacklaws felt his weight sag into the horse. There was a rustling, grunting sound, and another hog came nosing out of the brush from the direction of the reed bed. This was an immense blue sow, bigger than any they had seen so far, its sharp back as high as Mock's waist. It must have heard them first, or smelled them, for it halted abruptly, and its malevolent little eyes could not focus on them for a moment. Then it saw the two men, and a bestial sound shook its shaggy chest.

"Where is he, Kenny?" gasped Mock. "My head's spinnin' so I can't see a thing."

"It's a *she*, right in front of you," Blacklaws said, fighting the rearing horse. "That's blood dripping from her whiskers. If she's wounded, she'll be twice as dangerous. For God's sake, will you get that cotton out of your head and climb on!"

"I'm afraid to turn around, Kenny. Long as she thinks I'm looking at her, she won't charge. She'll rush me the minute I turn my back. I know these piney-rooters . . . !"

"Then hand me your gun," Blacklaws told him. "Mine's empty, and I can't reload and hold this horse at the same time."

"Lost my cutter in that fall, Kenny. You take off one way. I'll run the other. Maybe we'll mix 'em up so they won't know which way to go."

"With you so clabbered you can't see?" Blacklaws shouted, pulling the mare back down again. "You'd be spitted in a minute. Get my gun out of its holster, then, and reload it."

"You don't have to do this, Kenny. . . ."

"Get my gun, damn you!"

He felt Mock's hand pawing blindly for his holster, as the man hunted for the weapon without taking his face away from the giant sow. There was a tug, and the Remington was free. The mare squealed, fighting the bit. Blacklaws had to use both hands to hold the horse. They were directly between the two fiddling hogs. The boar guarding the dying razorback began tossing his head and throwing his chest back and forth. This sent the blue sow on the other side to grunting and coughing. Blacklaws knew the slightest thing would set off the beasts now. Smaller tugs came, as Mock found his belt and thumbed fresh shells free.

"I can't hold this bronc much longer, Mock. Can you see yet?"

"It's all fuzzy. That the sow over by the bindweed?"

"No," Blacklaws said. "You're way off. She's over in front of that palmetto. You'd better hand that gun up here when you've got it reloaded."

The sow was fretting around and gouging at the matted grass with her tusks, and Blacklaws knew she wanted to get over and help the boar protect their dying companion. A sweat-soured reek steamed up out of the whinnying horse, to mingle with the cloying odor of fresh blood and decaying brush.

"Mock . . . ," Blacklaws began. The sudden sound of his voice set the horse off again, and she tried to wheel away from Mock. Blacklaws put the reins hard against her neck to pull her back. The pull must have brought the bit too far up against the roof of the mare's mouth. With a wild scream of pain, she reared up. Throwing himself forward to stay on and beating at her neck to knock the animal down again, Blacklaws heard the sow's coughing roar and saw it rush Mock.

"Kenny!" yelled Mock. "Where is she?"

"The gun," shouted Blacklaws as the horse came down again. "The gun!"

Mock threw himself back against the mare's rump, his arm cast high above his head, holding the gun. This put it within Blacklaws's reach, and he forgot the horse in that moment to grab at the weapon. He seized it, as the horse started kicking savagely at Mock and spinning away. Fighting the frenzied mare with one hand, he had to twist around in the saddle to fire at the sow. He did not know how many bullets Mock had gotten into the gun. He only knew he shifted crazily, from one position to the other on that plunging horse, in order to keep firing at the sow's head until the gun was empty.

One of the bullets must have hit her brain, for she suddenly went down, snout plowing up the earth, and then flipped over into Mock, knocking him to his hands and knees. At the same time the other hog charged.

"Watch it, Mock!" shouted Blacklaws, trying to fight the frantic mare around in that direction.

Mock wheeled toward the grunts of the charging boar, striving to rise. But one of his feet was still caught under the heavy sow, and it tripped him back to his knee again. Blacklaws had gotten Tar Baby pointed toward Mock by now, and he dug spurs into the horse. The mare screamed and plunged directly between the charging boar and Mock. Blacklaws dropped the gun and leaned out of the saddle as he came above Mock. He caught him by the belt and swung him up off the ground. The weight of the man almost jerked him off. He pinched his legs, clinging desperately for another instant. He had a vague sense of the boar plunging past the rump of his horse.

Then he let go the reins to grab at the saddle horn with his free hand. He felt himself going over but still clung to Mock's belt, trying to squeeze a few more feet out of the ride. Then the combined weight of them sliding off on that side pulled the saddle itself under the horse.

Blacklaws released Mock and kicked free himself. They both hit the ground and rolled off into the brush with a great crash of bindweed and *agrito*. The bole of a cypress stopped Blacklaws. Everything seemed to spin about him with a roaring sound, and he hardly knew how he gained his hands and knees. He crouched there, shaking his head, until he could see through the flags and palmettos into the clearing. The boar had wheeled from its charge, staring around in bewilderment.

When he could not see them, he shook his head in savage little jerks and went to grunting and squealing and pawing the earth. Mock crept up beside Blacklaws, dabbing at his bleeding face. His vision must have cleared, for he watched the hog fixedly while it trotted around, sniffing the air. Both of them were hesitant to move, to speak, for fear of bringing the beast down on them again. Finally Blacklaws's bronc renewed her crashing romp through the thickets farther off. The boar wheeled that way, lifting his head to sniff, and then went trotting off, disappearing in the brush on the other side.

"Boy, howdy," whispered Mock. "I ain't been that close to things since I rode alligators with Jim Bowie. Do you know who that blue sow belongs to, Kenny?"

"I can see an earmark. I don't know whose it is."

"That's Teacup," whispered Mock. "That's Tate's pet hog. . . ."

Something stopped him. Blacklaws saw that his eyes had shifted to a farther point in the clearing. Finally Blacklaws made out a man standing hip deep in palmettos and bindweed, regarding the dead sow. It was Tate.

"Kenny," Mock said in a strained voice. "I hope to hell he didn't see you kill that sow."

Chapter Seven

It was raining again in Copper Bluffs. Rain dribbled off the *viga* poles of the adobe buildings and made glimmering channels down the ancient walls. Rain filled the wheel ruts lacing the streets and turned them to coppery rivers. Rain drummed soddenly into the splintered sidewalk fronting the newer buildings and lifted up the pungent reek of dampened pine.

Quintin Garland shook this sidewalk as he ducked from the meager protection of one wooden overhang to the next on his way to the stables. He had stayed late in his office, hoping the storm would abate, but was finally forced out when he saw it did not mean to stop. In front of the Clover Saloon he slowed down at the sight of a man down on his hands and knees, looking for something under the high sidewalk. Garland moved to the edge of the planks, frowning down at the slug-like figure till he recognized who it was.

"Mock," he said. "What's the matter?"

Mock's voice came indistinctly from underneath the planks. "I'm lookin' for Myrtle."

"Myrtle?"

"She got away from me. We were drinking in the Clover, and I must have said something that hurt her feelings. She hit me over the head with a pint of whiskey and ran out here."

"You're talking about your horse."

"That's right. Come 'ere, Myrtle. I didn't mean what I said." There was a scuffling sound under the planks and a jerk of Mock's broad rear. "Where are you, Myrtle? Come on out and I'll buy you another drink."

Garland reached down to grab the man by the seat of his pants and pulled him out. "You're drunk, Mock. You'll have pneumonia if you keep this up."

Mock bumped his head sliding back with Garland's angry pull. He came from beneath the high sidewalk to roll off hands and knees into a sitting position, leaning against the curb. A silly grin filled his face. Water dribbled down the greasy creases of his jowls.

"Sure I'm drunk," he laughed. "I'm never sober. Tried to get Kenny to come in and drink with me, but he wouldn't."

"Kenny . . . ?" Garland checked himself, frowning at the man. "You celebrating the hog hunt?" he asked. "It must have been a good one. King Wallace sold enough lard in town today to buy his liquor for a change."

"We killed seventy thousand hogs," chuckled Mock.

"Seventy thou . . . !" Garland stopped himself again. He smiled without much humor. "Sure. Seventy thousand. That's not many."

"It is when you count Teacup."

Garland leaned toward the man. "What?"

"Teacup, Teacup," Mock answered, his voice gaining volume. He threw up his arm dramatically. "I saddled her up and rode to Galveston. That's why Myrtle is so mad. She said it didn't befit my dignity to ride a hog. I will admit my feet dragged."

Garland stepped down into the mud, grabbing at Mock's shirt front and pulling him part way up. "Listen, you drunken liar, that isn't what happened. Tell me the truth. What about Teacup? Was Tate there?"

Mock swept Garland's hands off and, with inebriate dignity, tried to rise. He failed and had to turn around

72

and hug one of the supports of the overhang. He slid up this in careful, sinuous movements until he was erect. He stood there a while, leaning against it.

"Drunk, am I?" he said. "It's you who are drunk. You can't see the great truth in life."

Garland frowned intensely at the man. "Did somebody kill Teacup?" he asked.

"Even Pontius Pilate didn't know what truth was," said Mock.

"Did Kenny Blacklaws kill Teacup?"

Garland saw Mock's head lift slightly. His eyes were glazed as he stared at the post.

"Kenny Blacklaws?" Mock asked. Then, with startling violence, he whirled away, facing out toward the street. "If you see Myrtle, tell her I've gone home," he said and took one immense stride and fell onto his face.

Garland stood watching him a long moment, but Mock made no effort to rise. Then Garland himself returned to the sidewalk and walked to the stables, his whole mind taken up with the possibilities of this. He got his horse and headed out of town, heedless of the rain now. He followed the Houston Road till it turned northward to skirt the eastern fringe of the Big Thicket. A quarter mile up this he broke from the road on a meager trail that took him directly into the thicket itself.

Unlike the boggy country making up the bulk of Jefferson County, the thicket was a dry area, a veritable jungle of brushland that stretched north for a hundred miles. Most of it was completely unknown, except to the outlaws and fugitives who had sought its fastness as refuge. Garland himself had never been farther in than the few miles it took to reach Tate's place. With night blackening about him, he followed the narrow Indian trail through knee-deep masses of tossing palm fronds, mesquite clawing at his horse, brittle white brush rattling like old bones with his passage. He plunged into a grove of beeches and maples so dense and lightless he could not see his horse's ears. Finally he reached the wattle hut on the banks of a sluggish stream.

This was not the first time he had been here, for he had come to realize Tate knew this country as no other man did, and more than once he had used that knowledge to his advantage. He did not even have to call. The coughing sounds began, as the hogs sensed his horse. He could hear the beasts breaking from rain-drenched thickets about the hut, though he could not see them. There was a grunting chorus from within the hovel, and the door burst open.

Tate was holding a pine-knot torch, its eerie light flooding him and his hogs like ruddy paint. A half dozen of them banked up behind his legs, and a shoat tried to squeeze between his knees. The wind kept blowing fitful gusts of rain across the torch, and it spat and hissed, almost going out. He stepped farther back inside, holding the light directly above his head so that it cast his primitive face into macabre pockets of shadow.

"I was in town," Garland said. "Mock told me somebody killed Teacup."

Tate made some inarticulate sound deep in his chest, looking down at the ground and moving his head from side to side like a rooting hog. His eyes had a wild gleam in the flickering light.

"Blacklaws?" asked Garland.

"He oughtta be hung!" Tate threw his head back, and his voice left him in a shrill squeal. "He oughtta be strung up and swing like a loose gallus every time the wind blows. He knew Teacup was mine. He saw the earmarks on her. They always know, but they go right ahead and kill 'em anyway . . . don't care if it's old Tate's . . . go ahead and murder. Listen to 'em running away in the thickets . . . listen to 'em squealing, my little pigs, my Teacup . . . !''

He stopped for lack of breath, chest heaving. The childish fit had left his face hideous. With the rain making a kettledrum out of his hat, Garland leaned toward the man, speaking softly.

"You didn't have a price the other day, Tate."

The abandoned rage took a long time to leave Tate's face. Finally he rolled his head back till his eyes were on Garland, small and sly now with his own secret knowledge.

"And now," he said, "you think I *do* have a price."

"You have a reason. It was *your* hog he killed."

"Always the lawyer-man, ain't you. Always twisting it around so's it's old Tate and not you. Always putting things in my mouth. You want him dead as much as I do, but you won't admit it." He paused again, but Garland did not speak. Tate licked his lips. "All right. So I have a price. It's a latch."

"A latch?"

"A latch, a latch for a door, with a bolt, a strong bolt that'll take pounding, a nice shiny latch"—Tate chuckled—"but it won't stay shiny long in this country, will it? It'll rust up in a day, look like any other old latch. Nobody'll know the difference, not even somebody who always figures things out ahead."

Garland studied the man, with the implications of it running through his mind. "I'll have to get it in Copper Bluffs," he said.

"You're thinking that will mix you up in whatever I do with it," murmured Tate. He spat. "You're right. But that's my price."

Garland did not pause to weigh the ramifications of this, however dangerous it might be to him. He only followed the bitter urges within him.

"I'll get it for you," he said. "Tonight."

Chapter Eight

The Garland house lay half way between the Big Thicket and Copper Bluffs, some five miles west of town at the head of Bayou Lafitte. Martin Garland had built it here before the war, first trying to found a cotton empire only to be wiped out by the war, then trying to become rich in cattle, only to be blocked off from this by his death. It left the home nothing more than a simple dog-run structure, to mock the dreams of both Martin and his son.

Under Quintin's neglect the unpeeled cedar logs were rotting away and sagging at their dovetailed corners, the ashlar stonework of the chimney was slowly sinking into the ground, and the saddle roof was patched with tin or buckskin wherever the hand-split shingles had been beaten off by the winds. Usually this squalor brought a bitter depression to Garland, but tonight he was unaware of it, as he rode his Copperbottom around to the pole corral and let it in with the other gaunt mare, stripping the saddle off. He had gone back to Copper Bluffs to get Tate's latch. Though the store had been closed, Deller lived in the back of the building and could be persuaded to get what a man wanted. Garland had then taken the latch back to Tate and had finally come home.

The water dripping from him, he walked in through the rear of the covered breezeway that divided the two sections of the house and dropped his sodden saddle beside another kack, a pair of frayed saddle blankets, a rusty plow, and a heap of other gear. Taking his hat off and slapping the rain out of it against his slicker, he turned to the door on the right and reached for the latch. The portal swung open before he realized it was not latched. He stood there, with the sense of another presence in the darkened room.

"Who is it?" he asked sharply.

"Me, Quintin," answered Phil Manatte in a weak voice.

Garland stepped in, rustling for matches on the shelf, turning to light the hurricane lantern on the bare plank table. Its illumination spread out across a sagging puncheon floor, a pair of rawhide-seated chairs, a tumbled bed in one corner. Upon this sat Phil.

There was a smear of black mud on his jaw, and his clothes were blotched with it; he had left tracks of it from the door to the bed that still lay like viscid scars against the floor. He had his shirt opened and was holding a piece of filthy cloth wadded up inside, against his chest. Then Garland realized that some of the black spots on his shirt were not mud. He walked to the boy, grasping his shoulder.

"Why did you come here like this?"

"You've got to help me," the boy said. "My horse played out south of here, and I just couldn't make it home."

Garland's face sharpened. He wheeled and walked to the door, shutting and latching it.

"Now what is it?" he asked. "If you want me to help you, you've got to tell me. Did someone catch you peeling the wrong hide?"

Phil's whole body settled resignedly into the bed. "Yes," he said, "I guess they did."

"You weren't on your own, were you?"

The boy lifted his face in an effort of defiance. "Yes. I was. I was on my own."

"No you weren't!" Garland caught his shoulder again, bringing a spasm of pain to Phil's face. "You're working for somebody. The odds are building up against a man operating alone, unless he knows a place he can get rid of his hides quick. And the only place is that packery everybody's been looking for . . . isn't it?"

Phil shook his head dully. "I can't tell you, Quintin."

Garland pinched tighter. "Who are you working for, Phil?"

The boy's eyes squinted shut. "Please don't, Quintin, I can't tell you anything. I can't . . . !"

Garland released him, wheeling away to walk to the table and stand there. He could see Phil was near the breaking point. Unconsciously, he began to assume his courtroom manner. The stage pause. The dramatic gesture. The calculated timing. He let silence gather weight in the room. Wind-driven rain rattled at a loose shutter. Phil's breathing seemed to become more labored.

"You can't stay here," Garland said abruptly.

He heard Phil catch his breath then speak with heavy effort. "I don't think they're actually on my trail. I threw them off a couple of miles south. But they're in the district."

"Then you can't stay here. There's no place to hide you, Phil." Again that pause. "Where will you go?"

"I don't know, I don't know. . . ."

"Home?"

"I couldn't make it, Quintin."

"Then where?"

"Quintin, why won't you help me?"

"I'm trying to, Phil. You've got to meet me half way. As your friend, I want to get you out of this. But as a lawyer I can't go into it blind. I've got to know what the risks are. You must realize the position you put me in.''

''I do realize.'' Phil's voice was barely audible. ''I'm sorry.''

Garland turned to him, putting compassion into his words. ''Never mind, Phil. What's a friend for if it isn't to help in a time like this?''

''It wouldn't get you in trouble to help me get home,'' Phil mumbled. ''Just let me stay here tonight and then maybe help me home?''

''Don't you think they'll look there, too? If they suspect you at all, don't you think that's the first place they'll look? Do you want to drag your sister into this?''

Phil's face lifted sharply, pale and strained. He stared in wide-eyed protest at Garland for an instant. Then he dropped his head again.

''No,'' he said, pushing his hand sickly against the wound ''No, I couldn't do that. I couldn't drag Corsica into it.''

Again Garland let the silence run on, seeing it press the boy deeper against the bed. ''To be here longer than overnight would be dangerous, Phil,'' he said at last. ''You'll need someone to watch you. And if I didn't show up in town, it would arouse their suspicions. And if you can't stay here, and you can't go home, where can you go?''

It came out of Phil in a half sob. ''I don't know, Quintin, I don't know.''

''I want to help you, Phil. I'll be willing to take you anywhere you say. Anywhere, Phil.''

Defeat put a putty color into Phil's face, and his whole body seemed to shrink. ''All right,'' he said finally. ''I'll tell you where to take me.''

Triumph sharpened the angles of Garland's narrow face. The arrowhead shadows beneath his pointed cheekbones grew longer; his brows took on a greater peak.

His tall body inclined forward, waiting for Phil to go on. The boy finally sensed this and looked up, with a feeble anger washing through his pain.

"I can't tell you all the directions now. It's too complicated. We can't start till tomorrow anyway."

A ridge of whitened flesh jumped up about Garland's compressed lips. He turned away to hide his anger from the boy. Perhaps it would be a mistake to prod Phil farther. He had gotten enough from him for now.

At this moment one of the horses whinnied from out back. The light in the room revealed how surprise flashed across Garland's eyes with the upward toss of his head. Then he wheeled and went to the bed, sweeping some old rag rugs from beneath it to throw them over the muddy footprints on the floor. After this he got a fire going in the potbellied wood stove, working with a swift, nervous efficiency, and dragged a chair over for Phil, helping him into this.

"Sit as close as you can. Dry that mud on your pants. Get the shirt off quick."

He went to an old leather-bound trunk in the corner, taking out a fresh shirt. Phil had slipped from one sleeve of his own shirt, and Garland helped him strip the rest off. He saw that the wound was in the shoulder. He found a piece of clean cotton, folded it into a compress, then tore strips off of Phil's shirt to bind it. He helped the boy into his own shirt, getting a dipperful of water to wash his face and hands of mud. After this he took the bloody remnants of the shirt and picked up his own wet slicker and overcoat, taking them out into the breezeway and burying them beneath the gear there. Then he went back in and fished a bottle of whiskey and a pack of cards from the cupboard. He poured a big drink of whiskey for the boy and, while Phil drank this, took a handful of carefully hoarded coins from a pot and put it on the table. He fished out a couple of aces and three low numbers for his hand and gave Phil a seven, eight, nine, and a couple of face cards. Phil stared dully at them, a flush of new life filling his face from the whiskey.

"You think of everything, don't you?" he said.

The horse whinnied in the corral again. The excitement of it filled Garland's eyes with a bright glow. Think you can do it?" he asked.

"I'll try," Phil told him weakly.

At this moment there was the muffled sound of horses approaching, the suction of boots in mud. Then these boots clattered on the puncheon flooring of the breezeway, and the door shuddered beneath a knock.

Garland scraped his chair out and rose to open the door. Sheriff Waco Sheridan stood there with his deputy, Hack Cameron. Behind them were John Roman, Agate Ayers, and Louis Obermeier. Sheriff Sheridan was tall and stooped through the shoulders, as if from the weight of his official responsibilities. He had an undershot jaw and pouting lips that gave his face a pusillanimous look. Only a close study would reveal the searching quality to his eyes. They were held in a perpetual squint, from which a network of spidery wrinkles spread downward into the hollows of his cheeks, lending them a sucked-in appearance.

" 'Evening, Quintin," he murmured. His glance took in the whole room with one quick slice.

" 'Evening, Sheriff," answered Garland. He could still not hide the hostility in his eyes as they ran on to John Roman.

"Now you ain't going to let an old grudge clabber the milk, are you?" asked the sheriff.

"I can't help how I feel about some things," answered Garland. "But I guess I wouldn't leave a dog out on a night like this."

He did not miss the way Roman's mottled jowls

hunched up. He stepped back and allowed them to enter. Hack Cameron followed the sheriff, a younger man with black hair the rain had dampened till it lay against his temples and at the back of his neck in tight ringlets. The seriousness with which he took the office of deputy was in the sober lack of humor that lay heavily over his mahogany-colored face. Louis Obermeier followed. He was the biggest cattleman in the county, next to Roman—a man not much over five feet tall built like a beer keg, his short-cropped head as square as a blockhouse. He laid his eyes on Garland in a smileless way and pulled peevishly at a ruddy bulb of a nose.

Then it was Roman, the pelt of his bearskin coat turned curly by the rain, shaking the puncheon flooring with his aggressive weight. Agate Ayers followed him in, and that was all, though Garland could hear the muttering talk of other riders outside. The men grouped themselves loosely across the room, water dripping insistently from gleaming slickers onto the floor. Agate and the sheriff wore heavy mackinaws, the dampened lint glimmering faintly all over them. Garland saw the sheriff's eyes cross the floor, beneath their feet, and then raise to Phil.

"Stud?" he asked.

"Draw," Phil smiled.

Sheriff Sheridan shifted idly to the table, taking up the hand of cards Garland had put down and looked at them without letting Phil see. He pouted his lips in approval and lay the hand back, face down.

"On the trail of something, Waco?" Garland asked.

"What makes you think that, Quintin?" questioned the sheriff.

"You always get that hound-dog look, Waco. How about a drink to take the curse off this night?"

"Sounds good," answered the sheriff. "Been playing long, Phil?"

"Not long," answered Phil.

The heat was beginning to draw the rank smell of wet wool from the men now, as Garland moved over to the shelf and took some tin cups down. He poured a drink for the sheriff first. Sheridan accepted it and backed up to the bed, lowering himself onto this with a tired wheeze. He idly rubbed a forefinger down one edge of the blankets. Garland was pouring Obermeier's drink. He could not help that one look at Sheridan, when the man lifted his finger.

"Anybody else passed this way tonight?" Sheridan asked, raising his eyes suddenly to catch Garland watching him.

Garland dropped his glance quickly to the cup he was filling, but a sharp relief filled him. There had been none of Phil's blood on Sheridan's finger.

"We wouldn't have heard them if they did, in this weather," Garland said. "Hide rustlers, Sheriff?"

"What else?" asked Obermeier, glaring at the whiskey in his cup. "A couple of my boys come across a cut of my beef being run across Mexican Creek toward the Big Thicket. The rustlers got away, but we think one of them got clipped."

"Trail run past here?" asked Garland, handing out Roman's drink. The man took it in one gulp, letting his breath out afterward in a guttural sound of satisfaction. The sheriff's squinted eyes passed idly across Phil's pants leg.

"We lost the trail a couple of miles south," he said. "Thought you might be coming home about this time and seen somebody."

With the drinks passed out, Garland moved to the fire and bent to stoke another length of wood in. He let his own eyes pass over Phil's pants. Another settling of relief ran through him as he saw that the mud was almost dry on the cloth. When he straightened, he saw that

Sheriff Sheridan's glance had lifted from the pants to Phil's face.

"How's things over Manatte way, Phil?" he asked.

"Just fine, Sheriff, just fine," grinned Phil.

Garland wondered if the others could see the strained little lines about the boy's mouth. A silvery film passed across Phil's blue eyes, and Garland saw his hand lift to the table feebly, as if for support. Garland straightened swiftly, hoping his movement would draw their attention.

"Wish the place was bigger. The rest of your posse could come in."

Sheridan was building himself a cigarette and put his sack of tobacco on the bed while he rolled the smoke. "That's all right. We'll be going in a minute."

"How's things up Copper Bluffs way, Garland?" Roman asked.

Garland placed his back to the fire, spreading his legs out. "I guess you ought to know, Roman."

"Had any clients lately?" Roman asked.

"What's it to you?"

"Lawyer needs clients to keep him in business. That last client you had didn't do so well."

Garland's voice was growing thin. "He was innocent of both charges."

"The jury didn't think so." That carnal grin spread Roman's jowls. "But then you must have thought so to take him on. A lawyer never takes a case if he knows for certain his client is guilty, does he?"

"Guilty, innocent, what do you know about that?" Garland said thinly. "It's just how much Obermeier pays the jurors or how big Roman threatens the judge."

Agate made some sharp move away from the wall. Roman leaned toward Garland. "That sounds like an accusation . . . ?"

"That'll do, Roman," said Waco Sheridan. His voice

was not loud, but it cut off their sounds and movements sharply with its brittle authority. He rose and walked to the wall, striking a match down it. "We didn't come here for that," he murmured, lifting the ignited match to his cigarette. After lighting his smoke, he waved his match out and turned suddenly to Phil. "Did we, Phil?"

The boy had been staring at the floor with a glassy expression in his eyes, and he jumped faintly. "Yeah," he said. "Yeah."

"Yeah what?"

Phil's chin dug into his neck, and a chuckle shook him, surprising Garland. "You can't lock two fighting cocks in a pen without they start spurring at each other, Sheriff," the boy said.

A droll grin tilted Sheridan's pursed mouth. "No, I guess you can't." His eyes brushed a corner of the room. "I guess you can't."

Agate cleared his throat roughly, began to drum the fingers of one hand against his rawhide leggins. It made a nervous little tattoo in the room. Obermeier moved over to set his empty cup down, pulling at his nose. Garland saw minute beads of sweat breaking out across Phil's forehead. That last effort of concentration had taken a lot from him. Hack Cameron was studying the boy soberly. Garland knew he had to take their attention off Phil again. He realized that a man innocent of anything would have surely felt their suspicion by now.

"What are you looking for, Waco?" he said. "I never did think there was much sport playing a fish."

Sheridan raised his brows. "We weren't looking for nothing, Quintin. You have a guilty conscience?"

"Man wouldn't have to have a guilty conscience, the way the bunch of you are acting. Maybe you'd like to search the place for hides?"

Sheridan grinned. "Now don't get your neck swelled up. We'll be going. See anything, let us know."

He dropped his half-smoked cigarette, ground it out, nodded at the others. Hack Cameron turned to open the door, and Obermeier wheeled to follow. Roman did not move.

"This isn't finished, Garland," he said. "You can't go around making talk like that without somebody stomping your face in."

Garland's cheeks pinched in. "Would you call that a threat, Sheriff?" he asked.

Sheridan squeezed Roman's arm. "Take it easy, John. I don't want to hear either of you talking that way."

Roman stared at Garland a moment longer. Then he made a snorting sound and wheeled to stamp out, shaking the whole house. Sheridan smiled wryly at Garland, nodded to Phil, and went out. As Garland closed the door behind him, Phil let out a long sigh and started bending over to put his head on the table.

"Not yet," Garland said, whirling to him. "Hang on another minute. I know Sheridan. Hang on."

He straightened the boy up, poured him another drink. Phil's eyes looked like a sleepy child's, unable to focus. A little pulse beat raggedly in the hollow of his collarbone. Before Garland could lift the drink to his lips, the door scraped open again. He turned to see Waco Sheridan standing there.

"Forgot my Bull Durham sack," said the sheriff ruefully.

Garland set the glass down. "Yes," he said. "On the bed, I guess."

He turned to get it. With each step he waited for the sound of Phil's body sliding from the chair. He picked up the tobacco sack. The sheriff's boots scraped restlessly against the damp outer floor. Garland turned back. Phil was sitting stiffly in the chair, chin settled into his neck so deeply it left furrows of slack flesh.

"How's the family, Phil?"

The pause after that pounded against Garland's nerves. Then Phil raised his head, smiling. "Just fine, Sheriff. Drop in if you're out our way. Still some of that peach left."

Sheridan's lips shaped into a pouting smile. "That I will."

Those grained wrinkles formed their studying network about his eyes, as he took the sack from Garland's hand. He touched the dripping brim of his hat and turned to go out. Garland shut the door. He stood facing it till he heard the squeak of saddle leather. From behind him there was a faint gasp. Garland wheeled to see Phil slide out of the chair and onto the floor, unconscious.

Chapter Nine

The day after the hog hunt, Blacklaws rode to the coast. Carew had told him they had checked this section carefully, but Blacklaws wanted a look for himself. He could not go due south from his line shack; that would have taken him directly into Congo Bog. He headed east to the Sabine and followed the river, riding through a land laced with bayous and tangled with a twilit jungle of bindweed and catclaw and moss-hung cypress. He reached Lake Sabine before noon and followed its borders to Sabine Pass and thence to the sea. He rested his horse among the dunes, letting the refreshment of salt air and snowy surf fill him deeply.

Then he turned west, picking up the first deserted village within a couple of miles. This had been used by shrimpers in the early days, until a succession of hurricanes had driven them out. Now the forlorn hovels were half buried in sand, the palm thatching of their roofs long ago swept off.

There were only two logical channels by which the hide rustlers could market their stuff—overland to Galveston, or by sea to New Orleans and other eastern ports. If they did it by sea, this was the kind of place they would use, bringing the hides and tallow down here through the bayous on pirogues and flatboats and then hauling them out to a waiting schooner in surfboats. But Blacklaws found no fresh sign in the shrimp village.

He rode on west, coming across half a dozen more likely spots, none showing signs of recent use. The early afternoon sun was burning at his face when he reached the marsh. It looked to be the end of a bayou, crawling like a crooked finger a quarter of a mile from the surf, protected by sand that had banked up into dunes with pickle grass topping them like tousled jade wigs. It was here he found the fresh hoofprints. They were of two horses, walking along the marsh.

Tar Baby suddenly threw up her head and whinnied. Blacklaws straightened from his study. At the same moment a pair of riders lifted up over the dunes ahead of him and came to a sharp halt on top. One of them had an old Ward-Burton across his animal's withers, and he swung it around to cover Blacklaws. After that the three of them stared at each other for a tense space without speaking. The one with the rifle sat tall and slack in the saddle. A cynical knowledge of life lay in his weather-whipped face, and his smoky eyes reflected a careful watchfulness. He reached up a crooked thumb to shove his greasy Stetson farther back on curly yellow hair.

"You're not on free range now, stranger. This is John Roman's land."

Blacklaws shrugged. "Didn't know he'd spread this far east. How long you been working for him?"

"I'll ask the questions," answered the man. "My name's Lee Deff. This is Eddie Hyde."

"I'm Kenny Blacklaws."

There was silence after that. The wind whipped salt spray against the horses and filled them with new vinegar. But Blacklaws had not missed the change in both men's faces. The man Deff had called Eddie Hyde shifted restively in his rawhide-laced saddle. There was a gathered compactness to his body, and his face had the keen edge of a honed blade. The cords in his rope-scarred hands rippled nervously as he fiddled at the reins and then jerked his horse's head up with a sharp pull.

"What the hell," he said. "We going to take him in?"

"There's been too much hide rustling around here," Deff told Blacklaws. "Roman's had to start keeping strangers off his land. He'll want to know what you're here for, and I think you better tell him in person. Just lift your reins and line out along this marsh."

Blacklaws did as they asked without speaking. There was no particular reluctance in him, or anger; he might as well see Roman while he was down this way. The white shore broke up into dunes that formed a veritable labyrinth across the beach. The marsh became long fingers of stagnant water thrusting themselves down the troughs between these dunes. The stench began to reach Blacklaws before he saw the house. It grew so strong it almost gagged him. It was the compounded smell of rotten meat and blood and rendered tallow that always marked a packery. Most of the larger ranchers had been forced to skin their own hides and pack their own meat to make any profit out of what business was left to them.

Blacklaws wound out from between the dunes and saw the first pens. They were sprawled out across the beach, filled with the restless movement of bawling cattle. Nearer the water were three long slaughter shanties and a half dozen big wooden vats encrusted with dirty brine, where the tallow was rendered. A rickety pier ran out beyond the surf, and a couple of dories were drawn up above the high-water mark.

Then it was the house. It brought back the past poignantly. During the two years that Blacklaws's mother had been married to Martin Garland, she and Martin had often attended the cotillions given by Roman and his wife. Blacklaws and Quintin Garland had both come to play with the other children in the gardens while their parents danced in the great parlor.

The house still looked splendid from here, set up on the high bluff overlooking the sea, its six white columns gleaming like marble. It had been built early in the century by a cotton planter, who had sold it to Roman when Roman got rich driving cattle to the Louisiana markets. As Blacklaws drew nearer, however, he began to see the deterioration the war and the death of Roman's wife had wrought on the house. Azaleas and camellias had once spread their colorful profusion beneath the post oaks lining the winding drive; now only catclaw and *agrito* choked the space, reaching across the road in a thorny tangle. The white paint was peeling off the pillars, and their bases were mottled by a mold green with age and neglect. Most of the small panes in the fanlight above the door had been smashed out, to lie in glittering heaps of glass on either side of the portal.

Blacklaws dismounted at Deff's bidding. Both Deff and Hyde followed him across the porch, their boot heels making a dull clatter on the flagstones. Hyde opened the door. Again it was the impact of the past. The sixty-five-foot center hall thrusting its shadowed chasm through the length of the house had been Mrs. Roman's pride. Now the French hand-blocked wallpaper was peeling off in browning crusts, the Adamesque mirrors were cracked and filmed with dust.

From the parlor came the clink of glasses. Deff nodded for Blacklaws to turn in there. The room was heavily shadowed, even this early in the afternoon. Only one or two of the original velvet drapes remained, but soiled cheesecloth or dirty gunny sacking had been pinned up over the rest of the windows, cutting out much of the light. The remainder of the room reflected the same squalor. The great cut-glass chandelier had fallen from the ceiling, and the smashed bulk of it had been dragged into one corner, leaving its broken crystal pendants lying all around the room. The other corners were heaped with litters of bones and empty tin cans and castoff clothing and gear. It was a house in which back-country men had lived for a long time without the civilizing influence of a woman.

Gauche Sallier stood at the marble mantel, a half-emptied glass in one feminine hand. John Roman's bulk filled a wing chair before the hearth, its leather upholstery torn and scarred by cigar burns. Roman was in shirt sleeves, the cuffs rolled back off hairy forearms, and had been lighting a cigar when Blacklaws entered. The poor light made a circling gleam on his bald head as he turned to see who had entered.

"We found him up toward the pass," Lee Deff said.

Roman waved out the match just before it burned him, dropped it on the floor. He studied Blacklaws silently, a faint ripple of muscles working through his whiskey-veined jowls. Then he pointed the cigar casually at the man across from him.

"You know Harry Sharp?"

"Not formally," Blacklaws said. "I've heard of his Dollar Sign."

"This is Blacklaws, Harry," Roman murmured. "Martin Garland's stepson."

"Oh."

The word left Sharp in soft understanding. He was seated across from Roman, a tall man in an impeccably tailored steel-pen coat and fawn-colored trousers, a graceful indolence to the way he was sprawled on the divan. He had a sharp, angular face and a luxuriant head of red hair, with ruddy burnsides trained carefully against the gleaming line of his jaw.

Roman lit another match, drew on his cigar till it was going, then let out a stream of smoke. "I suppose Deff told you how picky I am about anybody riding my pastures," he said.

"Times have changed," Blacklaws said.

Roman spat a piece of the cigar wrapper over the side of the chair. "I know what you're thinking. You're right. Having everybody in Jefferson County swarming over this place was Missus Roman's doings. She's been dead seven years now, Kenny, and I'm just a crusty old bachelor without the softening influence of a woman."

He paused, staring beyond Sharp out the windows. For a moment Blacklaws saw a tiredness in the man. He had not thought of Roman in this light—an aging old bull who had lost the one soft and beautiful thing in his life, and who knew his moments of bitter loneliness. Then Roman broke the mood, swinging his scarred head around sharply.

"Taken any more Double Sickle stuff?"

"Haven't come across any dead ones," Blacklaws said.

"That right, Gauche?" asked Roman.

"As far as I know, *m'sieu.*"

"How about the live ones?" Roman said.

"You know what I told you about that," Blacklaws said.

"You wasn't in on last night's rustling, then?"

"Somebody pick up a cut of stuff last night?"

"Obermeier's stuff," Sharp said indifferently. "Rustler got wounded in the fight, and they followed him as far as Bayou Lafitte."

"How could you trail him in that rain?" Blacklaws asked.

"We didn't trail," Roman muttered. "We were close enough to follow the man. A couple of Obermeier's riders come across the rustlers at work and clipped one of them. An Obermeier man followed the wounded rustler while the other tailed it for Obermeier's house. I was visiting the old Dutchman. We sent a man after the sheriff and then took out. The Obermeier man tailing the rustler tore his whole damn' shirt up, leaving pieces of it hooked on trees for us to follow. We picked him up near Bayou Lafitte. He'd lost the rustler and his sign too." Roman tilted his bald head back, looking up at Blacklaws. "You weren't down by Bayou Lafitte last night, were you?"

"Would you like to stand on your feet and say that?" Blacklaws said.

Roman's eyes widened in surprise, spreading their pawky pouches. Then he leaned forward with a grunt, grabbing the arms of the chair and spreading his boots to take his weight.

"Oh, don't be a fool, John," Sharp said disgustedly. It stopped Roman, bent forward this way. His eyes swung from Blacklaws to the other man. Sharp shrugged impatiently. "What did you expect?" he asked. "No honest man is going to let you imply things like that. At least not any man with sand in him. You're getting an obsession about this thing. Not everybody in the world is a hide rustler."

Roman remained in the same position, with his eyes switching back to Blacklaws, squinted almost shut now. Then he settled back into his chair, chin sinking into his chest, and stared moodily ahead of him for a moment.

He threw back his head so suddenly it startled Black-laws. That guttural laugh filled the room then dwindled off to a row of chuckles that shook Roman's beefy belly.

"You looked ready to tromp me, Kenny. I thought you couldn't be prodded."

Blacklaws spoke without heat. "I'm just tired being called a rustler, Roman. Don't do it again."

The coarse humor had left Roman again, and he was staring ahead of him that way once more without seeming to see Sharp, his pawky eyes barely visible behind slitted lids.

"Kenny," he said, "I'll do what I please, when I please. I wouldn't advise you to be found on my land again." He looked up at Blacklaws, as if expecting some answer. When Blacklaws gave none, he slapped the arm of his chair with a callused palm. "All right," he snorted. "Have a drink before you go, anyway."

"It's a long ride back. I'd better get started."

Roman's shrug was surly. "Suit yourself."

As Blacklaws turned to go, his gaze swung across Gauche Sallier. The Creole was watching him intently from those sooty eyes.

"How right you are, *m'sieu*," Sallier said. "It is a long ride back . . . *n'est-ce pas*?"

Chapter Ten

Though spring was near, the inevitable fogs of winter still rolled in off the coast and steamed up out of the bayous, saturating the countryside with a pearly mist in which the underbrush and timber swam like the rootless vegetation of some mysterious underworld. The moisture gathered densely on everything, beading branch and foliage so heavily that the whole forest seemed to have broken out in a jeweled sweat. The fog sucked up color, robbing the land of definition and hue until the trees and bayous and rises and hollows blended into one dream-like tapestry that floated eerily past the eye like a ghostly memory.

To some it would have been moody and depressing, but to Corsica it was only another fascinating phase of this place she loved. The unique loneliness of the fog seemed to bring her closer to the land itself. She welcomed the sense of merging her identity with the sad cypresses and the ancient post oaks that crept mistily past her as she let her horse pick its way along the river road.

Her pleasure in the land, however, was not as keen as usual. Worry about Phil preoccupied her. He had returned from the hog hunt with Dee, both of them loaded down with side meat and lard. Dee had taken the wagon back to Rouquette's to get the rest of the meat, but Phil had gone into town. He had not returned that night or the next day. Now, on the second morning of Phil's absence, she was riding to Blacklaws's, hoping he might have an idea where the boy was.

She wore her fawn-colored riding habit, its draped skirt faithfully outlining the nubile curve of her hip and thigh against the saddle leathers. The tailored jacket only partly obscured the striking fullness of her breasts, and the pork-pie hat, blue as her eyes, sat jauntily on the back of her glossy coif, the soft feather in its brim ruffling against the nape of her neck at her slightest movement.

As she turned off the river road onto the cattle trail that led to Smoky Canes, she found her worry about Phil subdued by a strange new mixture of emotions. As before, she found it hard to separate or define the feelings that came with thought of Blacklaws. There was that obscure mingling of reluctance and eagerness she had felt the first night. Only the reluctance seemed sharper, after what had happened between Garland and Blacklaws. *Was Quintin right? Had Blacklaws really killed Martin Garland? And if he had—even if the killing had been self-defense or an accident in a fight—how should she feel? She could not find any condemnation in her. Yet, after seeing Garland and Blacklaws together the other night, it was obvious the two of them could not be reconciled. And if she were to stand by Quintin's side, as a woman in love should, she would have to cut all the ties that bound her and Blacklaws.*

She found angry revolt rising up in her at this. *It wasn't fair. It was small of Garland.* Then she tried to block this off. *Why should it cut so deeply? Kenny had been gone nine years. They had only been kids when he left. Why should she feel this way?*

This train of thought put her in such a sudden turmoil that she was afraid to analyze her feelings any further, and she lifted her horse into a canter. *Maybe she was wrong. Maybe they could be reconciled.* She clung to this thought as she went on down the trail to the cutoff. This took her into the dense stands of loblolly pines and eventually into the salt-grass meadow by the canes. She saw that the corral was empty. She hitched her horse and found the door unlatched and went in anyway and stood there a long while, looking around the room. As old and dilapidated as the shack was, it had a neat, ordered appearance. It made her think of Blacklaws's mind and brought her very close to him for a moment, cleansing her of those bitter thoughts and leaving only the picture of him which she wanted to remember. Despite all the precision of detail there would never be any sense of pettiness to the order connected with Kenny. More a feeling of spiritual bigness that could profit by the practical capacities of his mind without letting these capacities fetter or narrow him.

She was still standing there when she heard her horse whinny and turned to see him through the doorway, swinging off Tar Baby. His heavy shoulders dragged a little, and a tired gauntness deepened the lines about his mouth and made his face look older, till he smiled. She could not help reacting to the infectious warmth of that smile.

"Not often I have such a distinguished guest," he said, coming in.

"Not often I get out, the way Dad is," she answered. "You look like you've spent the night in a barn."

He grinned ruefully. "Not quite a barn. Been down to the coast. Didn't get back in time and had to camp out. Have a seat, and I'll rustle up something to eat."

He shrugged out of his grimy ducking jacket and, without closing the door, took up the half-filled bucket and filled the coffee pot. Setting this on the stove and lighting the fire, he then rolled up his sleeves and proceeded to wash in the remaining water. This drew his shirt taut across his back, and she watched the faint curl and ripple of quilted muscle through the cloth. There was something sensual about it. She wondered if that was the feeling a man got from watching a woman.

"I really came down to ask you if you'd seen Phil," she said. "He left the evening of the hog hunt for town. He hasn't been home since."

"Haven't seen him since the hog hunt. Isn't the kid getting old enough to take a little ride by himself once in a while?"

"He always tells me where he's going," she said. "Nobody in town has seen him. I went to Sheriff Sheridan's office, but he was out."

"Mock's?"

"I don't think Phil knows the way to Mock's. The deepest into Congo Bog either of the boys has ever been is Chenière Dominique."

"How about hunting? Phil's coon dogs gone?"

She shook her head. "Josh and Moe were killed last December. That was when Phil and Dee saw Chenière Dominique. They were shot at. Both dogs were killed before they got out."

"How did they get that far into the bog in the first place?"

Corsica shrugged. "Chasing a 'coon, I suppose. Probably couldn't stop the dogs."

He turned from washing and went to get a towel. His gaze found hers and held it a moment. Then he turned away sharply, wiping his hands, to get coffee off the shelf. He slid the boiling water off the fire and measured the Triple X into the pot by guess, his back toward her.

"Kenny," she said, "do you still think I brought you and Quintin together deliberately the other night?"

He shrugged. "What does it matter?"

"*Something* is between us," she said.

"Time sometimes puts a gulf between people," he

replied. "A person changes a lot in nine years."

"You have, Kenny. I couldn't decide what it was the other night. Now I think I know. You were always a self-contained boy. Not many people understood you. But you still had emotions, and you showed them. Especially to me. You showed anger, and fear, and happiness, and sadness. You weren't afraid of emotions then."

"And now," he said, "you think I am?"

"I know you are," she answered. "That wasn't just anger you felt with Quintin the other night. You were afraid."

"Of Quintin?" he asked ironically.

"Of course not. You were afraid of yourself. Of that anger. Afraid you wouldn't be able to control it. Isn't that true?"

"You seem to know."

"Kenny, why won't you trust me?"

He turned to her, eyes somber and withdrawn. "Have I any reason to trust you?"

A hurt expression started forming in her face. She blanketed that off, settling back in the chair, speaking deliberately.

"In my closet is a whip. It has Martin Garland's name on the stock. I found it hidden in my father's room two years ago. I tried to get the story, but you know how Dad is. He says he can't remember." She bent toward him. "It's a clue in the mystery of a man's murder, and by rights I should have turned it in. But it's one of the things that would link you with Martin's death. Everybody knew how often Martin took you down there to whip you. I haven't turned it in. Now, won't you trust me?"

For just a moment she saw defense shred in his eyes. Then he turned away from her and moved to the door, staring out into the foggy meadow.

"Kenny, if the killing was accidental, who can blame you? It's easy to figure out what happened. Martin took you down there to whip you. There was a fight. You didn't mean to kill him. Who'd condemn you for that? If that's what happened, you're a fool for letting it stand between us."

He still did not turn around. She stared at the broad planes of muscle in his neck, beneath the shaggy edge of his black hair, holding the grain and camber and strength of an oak. She took a resigned breath.

"All right. I don't blame you for not trusting me. Even if the killing was accidental, I suppose you're smart in not admitting anything. There isn't enough evidence to convict you the way things stand. Keep your mouth shut and you're a free man. But that won't help what's happened inside. You feel anger with Quintin, and you're afraid. What are you afraid of where I'm concerned, Kenny?"

He spoke tightly. "You seem to know all the answers."

She settled back, studying him through half-lidded eyes. "You're afraid of anger. I think you're afraid of all your other feelings, too."

He did not answer, but the heavy cord at the side of his neck swelled with tension. She found herself leaning forward in a poignant desire to help him.

"Agate got drunk the other day and told around town about the fight you had with Roman and Sallier over the hide," she told him. "Agate said you didn't get very mad. That seemed to stick in his mind. An ordinary man would have gotten mad if they prodded him like that. But you didn't. Is it that way with everybody else? You've gotten yourself so under control that nobody can make you mad . . . except Quintin."

He did not answer yet, but the cord was standing out so heavily now she could see the pulse beat in it.

"Quintin is Martin's son. There's always been that hatred between you. He was so closely identified with Martin and all that happened. Has he become sort of a symbol, Kenny? You see Martin all over again . . . in Quintin?"

"Corsica . . . !"

Triumph brought her up out of the chair, as she saw how she was scoring. "What happens when we're kids leaves a bigger impression than we realize. Especially something as awful as that. You feel so guilty it's scarred your life. It's made you afraid of the anger that led you to kill Martin Garland. And Quintin's become a symbol of the whole thing. You're afraid he'll goad you to fighting again, and you're afraid you'll do the same thing with him you did with Martin. You keep remembering the way Martin looked, lying there with his face so beaten in nobody could recognize it. . . ."

He turned so sharply it cut her off. She stared up at his face in a fascinated way, waiting for him to speak. His eyes had that squinted, whipped look she had seen the night Garland had goaded him. But there was something else in them she could not identify. A frown was pulling his black brows together.

"What did you say about Martin's face?" he asked.

"I didn't see him. The doctor told us how badly he was beaten. What's the matter, Kenny?"

His withdrawal was as palpable, as if he had stepped back from her, though he had not moved. "Nothing," he said.

"Kenny," she said breathlessly, "won't you even admit it now I told you the killing wouldn't stand between us if it was accidental? It's what happened inside you that's between us. You always did live in your mind more than the rest of us. But you can't live there completely. It's not natural. You can't drain yourself of emotions. You might control them, but you can't stop feeling things completely . . . !''

"Can't I?'' His voice was brittle.

"Can you?"

It left her on a breath. Her whole body had risen toward him in her demand, till her breasts were against his chest. She felt the tremor run through him. Another expression broke through the withdrawn bleakness of his squinted eyes, filling them with something primitive and insupportable. His arms went about her, and her breasts flattened against his chest. His lips came down to hers.

She did not know how long it lasted. When he let her go, and she pulled back, they were both breathing heavily. She stared up at him with a chaotic mind. Dimly she knew she should feel anger. Dimly she knew the proper thing to do would be to slap him or let him know somehow that he had done wrong. But what was happening inside her went beyond propriety. She reached out toward him with her hands, and once more his arms went about her. She helped him as much as she could in their passion, and then they were on the floor, and he was inside of her.

Afterwards she rolled away from him, rose to her feet, gathering her undergarments. She turned and went blindly out the door to her horse, stuffed her undergarments beneath her skirt, and mounted. She wheeled the roan across the meadow. She was still unable to think when she reached the trees. She turned to look at his heavy-shouldered figure, now standing in the doorway, staring after her. She tried to see the expression on his face, couldn't, and realized it was because of the tears in her eyes. She turned the horse and kicked it into a dead run down the trail.

Chapter Eleven

After Corsica had gone, Blacklaws went back inside and sat down. For a long while no clear thought would come to him. He only knew how shaken he was by his desire for her. He had been helpless before it. All the control he had cultivated through the long years had been swept away by it.

Dimly he saw the danger of that. The emotion he felt for her fell in the same category as what he felt for Quintin. To him it was as much a weakness as drink or gambling and could ruin a man as surely. Perhaps she was right. Perhaps his fear of anger stemmed from a deep-rooted sense of guilt. He had realized that much himself. And perhaps his struggle against that fear had only complicated it, till he mistrusted all his emotions. But he knew the fear he had of his feelings for Corsica didn't arise completely from that night nine years ago. Part of it was right now.

For a moment there he had been on the verge of telling her the whole ugly picture of Martin Garland's death. The maternal concern, the sympathy, the compassion he had seen in her had drawn up a need for release so great it gagged him. That was natural. A man couldn't keep something like that to himself for nine years—hiding it, repressing it, running from it, dreaming about it at night—without building up an awful pressure. He had been close to telling before. But never so close as with Corsica. That's why it was a weakness. That's how it could ruin a man.

If I trusted her and told her about Martin Garland, how long before I told her why I really came back? That's the next logical step, isn't it? And what if I told her? Do I know yet where she really stands? It looks more than ever as if Phil's mixed up with the rustlers. How do I know it's only Phil? I'd be a fool to trust her. I almost ruined everything.

He rose in an insupportable restlessness, trying to order his thoughts. But they swam wildly in his head. Now it was what she had said about Martin's face.

How could he have been beaten that way? he thought. *Martin hit his head on a rock when he went down. That couldn't have messed his face up. I didn't hit him after he went down. Or did I?*

That stopped Blacklaws's restless pacing for a moment. Could his rage have been so deep that he didn't remember? He forced himself to try and recall other details of that night. Some came. Some wouldn't. He tried to thrash it out for a while and got so knotted up he had to quit. He tried to drive it from his mind as he made breakfast.

Something else began pushing him now, as he ate. Last night he had tried to reach Mexican Creek, where Roman had said the rustling took place. But his horse had played out, forcing him to halt near midnight. For his ride to the coast he had taken only enough food for two days, and this morning he had detoured back to his line shack for more supplies. He meant to try and pick up that sign of the rustlers, cold as it would be, and follow it out—that might take several days.

After adding more coffee and beans and bacon to his saddle roll, he took it out and lashed it on behind the cantle along with his coffee pot and frying pan. Then he lined out westward along the cattle trail. His mind was still so filled with Corsica that he failed to keep his usual sharp attention on the trail. Now he was beginning to wonder about Chenière Dominique. Corsica had said Phil and Dee had been shot at down there. It was a definite clue. Had it been unintentional on her part? Or had she planted it in his mind deliberately?

She had an uncanny knowledge of him, and the way his mind worked. She'd know what mention of something like that would do to him. But why would she do it deliberately? And what significance could it have? Did she want to drive him to the place or away from it?

He came to a turn in the trail, and it swung his vision around till a corner of it picked up the horsebacker following him about twenty feet behind. He reined up sharply, wheeling his bronc.

"I'd've been Quintin Garland, I could have cut you down, and you'd never know who did it," chuckled Charlie Carew, riding unhurriedly on up. "First time I ever seen you off guard, Kenny. You must have been thinking hard."

Again it seemed to Blacklaws as if his feelings for Corsica had betrayed him. He tipped his head toward the trees, and they rode through a pair of cypresses, brushing aside the clammy moss that hung from gnarled branches until they reached a glade hidden from the trail.

"Hear you killed Tate's pet hog," said Carew, pulling up.

"It would have killed us."

"I'd hate to be on that crazy Tate's list," Carew said. His cigar bobbed up and down with the words. Then he clamped his teeth shut, tilting it upward, and squinted shrewdly at Blacklaws. "What's on your mind, Kenny? It looks tough."

Blacklaws turned Tar Baby to face the detective's whey-bellied mare and then rode in till he was knee to knee with Carew. "You didn't tell me about Martin Garland's face, Charlie. All beaten in with a rock, so he could hardly be recognized.''

Carew frowned in a puzzled way. ''I didn't think I'd have to, Kenny.''

Blacklaws reached up suddenly to grab the man's shirt by the collar, twisting his fist in the cloth till the collar dug into the slack folds of Carew's neck. Carew caught spasmodically at Blacklaws's wrist, but Blacklaws lifted him up out of the saddle.

''Tell me just what you know, and just what you don't know, Charlie. I'm tired of this dirty little game you're playing.''

''You're choking me, Kenny. Let me down. Why should I bring up Martin's face? You'd know.''

''Would I?'' Blacklaws let him settle into the saddle, without loosening his grip. Carew was gagging, and sweat greased his face. ''What about the whip?'' Blacklaws asked.

''I told you we had it.''

Blacklaws lifted him upward again. ''You're a liar.''

''All right. You're choking me, Kenny. All right. We don't have it.''

''What about the man who saw Martin Garland killed?''

''You can't expect me to tip my hand so soon. Kenny . . . !''

''Was it Troy Manatte?'' Blacklaws twisted and lifted.

''All right,'' gasped Carew. ''Let me down. Troy Manatte.''

Blacklaws dropped him back into the saddle, still not releasing him. ''Troy couldn't have told you anything that would stand up in court. He can't even remember what he did yesterday. You just got to talking with him and pieced a few things together. You haven't got any man who saw Martin Garland killed. I ought to bust your guts.''

He released Carew with a disgusted sound. Carew removed his cigar, rubbing at his neck with the other hand.

"Never knew you was that strong, Kenny," he muttered. Then his sly humor returned, with effort. "Thought you was the man who wouldn't get mad?"

Blacklaws drew in a heavy breath. "I'm not mad at you. I wish I was. It would help."

Carew shook his head sadly, putting the cigar back in his mouth. "Detecting's a dirty game, Kenny. And now you're going." He waited for Blacklaws but, when no answer came, Carew murmured, "I offered you a hundred and fifty a month in the letter. How about two hundred?"

Blacklaws was staring blankly at the trees and hardly heard the man. "Charlie," he said, "what about Phil Manatte?"

Carew frowned at him. Then that chuckle began to shake the detective's pouchy belly. His lips spread back with it, while his teeth still clamped down on the cigar.

"I should have known, Kenny. Corsica's the reason you came back in the first place. And now that you've seen the trouble she's in, you can't step out."

"What about Phil?" asked Blacklaws doggedly.

Carew shrugged. "Nothing definite. Roman and Sheridan were hot on the trail of a wounded hide rustler the night of the hog hunt. His trail ran near Garland's place. They stopped in and found Garland and Phil playing poker. Sheridan said he was suspicious at first, but everything looked all right."

"Why should Garland shield Phil?"

"You're assuming Phil is one of the rustlers?"

"For argument's sake," Blacklaws said. "From two sources I've heard that Garland has passed word he has something which will enable the rustlers to take as many hides as they want, and Roman or Obermeier won't be able to touch them.''

Carew shook his head admiringly. ''That's what I meant when I said you could get things a man connected with the law couldn't, Kenny. I never heard anything like that.''

Blacklaws was still looking beyond Carew. ''Say the rustlers haven't taken Garland up. Garland still wants to contact them. He says he'll help Phil if Phil will lead him to that hidden packery. Add up?''

''Sounds logical.''

''If Phil's in it, I want to know why, Charlie. Has the Association got any connections in Houston or New York that would enable them to check up on the Manatte investments and how they're doing?''

''We can do that. Anything else?''

There was a protracted silence, in which Blacklaws sat straight-arming his saddle horn and leaning his weight against it, staring past Carew at the thickets. Chewing on his cigar, Carew squinted at Blacklaws.

''Hate me, Kenny?''

Blacklaws focused his eyes on the man, speaking in a low voice. ''I don't really know how I feel toward you, Charlie.''

Something sly entered Carew's eyes. ''You're not free of the brush yet, Kenny. Remember, if Garland got the slightest evidence in his hands, he'd have a warrant out for you that minute. It would be a slim case, but he'd push it. He's a smart lawyer and a dangerous man, for all the beating he's taken from Roman, and he's just as liable to get a conviction as not. And that whip is still evidence. . . .''

''Don't get carried away with yourself, Charlie.'' Blacklaws leaned toward the man, his voice softening. ''And don't use this to threaten me again.''

Carew's eyes widened faintly, staring at Blacklaws.

Then he seemed to become aware that he was chewing his stogie. He pulled it from his mouth, flinging it away with a disgusted snort. "Damned things," he said. "Oughtta take up chewing tobacco."

Chapter Twelve

Leaving Carew behind him, Blacklaws pointed Tar Baby westward once more along the cattle trail. For many miles it was a twilit journey through an exotic land of swamp and bayou. Finally he broke from this into the salt-grass prairies and came upon one of Obermeier's snake fences, following its meandering course for some distance. He never caught sight of the house, but the nauseating odors of the slaughtering pens reached him, for Obermeier stripped his own hides and salted his meat, just as John Roman was now doing and most of the other big operators in the region.

There had been no mention of exactly where along Mexican Creek the rustling took place but, if it had been Obermeier's beef, it would be somewhere in the vicinity of his pastures. Blacklaws passed the extreme western margins of the Obermeier land and rode on, till he struck the creek then turned northward through the meadows and timber banding this water, hunting for the tracks in the more open spots where cattle would browse. The rain had blotted out most of the ground sign, but finally he found where a big cut of beef had been pushed hard through a stand of timber, chipping off bark and leaving patches of hair in the thorny brush. He got the general direction of the run by this. It headed across Mexican Creek at a ford. He found more sign leading him to the Neches and a second ford here. Coming out on the other side of the river now, his mind began to work. Corsica was out of it, and Carew; and he began to concentrate on this, picking up all the signs and adding them and dividing them and placing them one against the other till the right answers came out.

It had always seemed strange to Blacklaws that the rustlers so consistently left a trail leading into the Big Thicket. The thicket was a logical place for the hide factory to be. There was enough unknown country in there to hide a dozen illegal packeries so completely they would never be found. It was a good risk of death for any lawman to penetrate the thicket too deeply, even in numbers. Yet it still seemed odd that rustlers clever enough to elude the law so long would advertise their hide-out so blatantly.

It put something in his mind. He was always one to look for sign other than the obvious. Now that habit began to focus itself, as he followed the meager sign of this trail.

It stopped raining about eight o'clock on the night of the rustling, he thought. *My only chance is that they were still running when the storm quit.*

Rain had washed out the tracks west of the Neches. Blacklaws barely hung on by much circling and studying of the brush and timber. About a mile west of the river he came upon a strip of white cloth stuck on a bush. He remembered what Roman had said about the Obermeier rider tearing up his whole shirt to leave sign the posse could follow. This must have been where the wounded rustler turned off, then, and the Obermeier rider after him. Rain had blotted all the ground sign out here too, and that strip of cloth was all Blacklaws had to go on.

He did not turn off here but headed west, following the main bunch in another mile of painful search for sign. Then suddenly he found tracks on the ground. *The rain stopped here*, he thought. *And these are the rustlers and the steers. Prints of both horses and cattle, far apart as they can stretch. That means they were still running like hell. What are these overlapping prints then? They look all shod, and they're walking. There's that bad caulk on Hack Cameron's right front. Won't he ever get it fixed? Sheridan must have sent Cameron and a few men after the bunch while the sheriff and Roman turned off after that wounded rustler.*

Blacklaws followed the trail on westward toward the Big Thicket. Now, with ground sign to read, he was watching the edges of the trail even more closely for a turnoff. He found one within another mile. It was a single man, prints far apart. One of the running rustlers. Blacklaws put it in the back of his mind without following the prints. He wanted something else besides this. He didn't actually know what it was, yet he knew this didn't fill the bill. He went another half mile, on foot now and leading Tar Baby, taking infinite pains to pick up all the sign along the edges of the trail. A man not half expecting it would never have seen it. He almost went by it himself. There was no sign on the ground. It was a patch of hide on a tree that caught his eye.

Red and white and speckled. Looks like a sabina steer. Too far off to be the main bunch. Had they turned some of the beef off here? Looks like erased prints on the ground. The whole bunch would have left more sign than this. So only part of the steers were turned off here by a couple of men, and the sign blotted out so good that a man following wouldn't find it, unless he was looking for it. The posse hadn't found it. They had gone right on by, following that main bunch up the trail toward the Big Thicket.

111

Blacklaws went in that direction too. A few hundred yards on he found a spot where another small cut of steers had been turned off into the trees. It was on a rocky ledge, where they would leave little sign. But Blacklaws had been watching for it, and a broken length of brush spotted it for him. However, he still followed the main trail till he came to a point where yet a third cut of steers had been turned off. This time he followed them. Within the timber the riders had quit trying to hide sign. It led him away from the main trail at right angles for half a mile then turned back toward the river. This sign joined the sign of the second small bunch that had been turned off, then the first bunch, and all three groups were driven together till they reached the river and put right down into the water.

Blacklaws sat his horse here, seeing the pattern now. Only a few cattle of the original bunch would be left, spread out to make it look as big as the bunch had first been, leaving a false trail for the posse that led right into the Big Thicket. Once inside it would not be hard to scatter and leave the posse at the end of their sign while actually the major portion of the original steers had been diverted off the trail long before reaching the thicket, a small group at a time, at places where it would not show, to be gathered together again in timber and then be driven back to the river. And then where?

North along the Neches was Sharp's Dollar Sign and beyond that the eastern fringe of the thicket itself, a hundred miles of river and jungle in which they might have turned up out of the water at any point. It was a hopeless job for a single man to find that point soon enough to do him any good. And south? About as hopeless. Fifteen miles of swampland, a big part of it the western edge of Congo Bog.

But Blacklaws felt no great defeat. He had found one of the things he wanted—the pattern of their operations.

It was a clever scheme for all its simplicity. The very fact that the Big Thicket was the most logical place in this country to hide an illegal packery had been one of the big points in their favor. They had consistently made it appear as if they were driving the cattle into the thicket, until everyone took it for granted that the hide factory was there. Then they had been free to turn the majority of their rustled stock into the waters of the Neches or the Sabine or a nearby bayou, driving it through the shallows for miles to leave no sign and eventually take the beef wherever they chose.

Blacklaws went back to the trail till he came to the place where the wounded man had turned off. He did not even stop here. If Sheridan and the posse had been unable to find that man, he would have little chance now. He rode on to where the second man had turned off. This was different. None of the posse had followed this one. Blacklaws wanted to know where he had gone.

It was a more exacting job now. Following the tracks of one man was hardly comparable to following sign left by a running herd. Often he lost the trail and had to stop and circle to pick it up again, the circle sometimes widening till it had a mile's diameter before he picked up the tracks once more. It took all his skill and patience, leading him ever southward, paralleling the river for some miles then crossing to head eastward till he was out of sight of the Neches. The sun was low now, casting its light obliquely through the tangled growth to throw long shadows that fluttered grotesquely across the tired man and his horse as they pressed on. Finally he reached what he thought was the southern section of Bayou Lafitte. The trail led down the bank of a ford here, and he splashed across, picking up sign easily on the other side. He halted, however, getting down.

There was something different here. In tracking, a man looked for some unusual conformation of hoof or shoe to distinguish his quarry—a back hoof that ran over on the outside or a distinctive imprint of one nail sticking farther out from the shoe than the rest. The animal Blacklaws was following possessed nothing unusual in the prints it left. Yet he was filled with the sense of something changed. He searched the tracks on this side for the reason for it. He looked back across the bayou. Why should he feel this way? They went in over there and came out here. It could be no other horse. He rose, putting it down to his own tension, mounted again, and once more took up the trail.

The woodlands became more dense and luxuriant, cypress swamps appearing on either side of the trail, woodbine and Virginia creeper and bindweed choking the post oaks and writhing across the solid ground in a tangled mat. The cloying scent of swamp flowers mingled with the rotten odors of bayou mud. Oxbow lakes began to appear, crescent-shaped sections of the river that had been cut off in earlier times to leave curving bodies of water covered with impenetrable masses of hyacinths so thick in some places they could bear a man's weight. Then the first *chenière* appeared. These were ancient barrier beaches, formed when the ocean covered this section of the land, built of shells piled up by the wind through centuries. When the ocean receded, it had left these ridges of crushed shells behind. With the forming of the swamps and bayous, the shell ridges that remained above water became islands, collecting sand and earth through the years till they would support undergrowth and timber. Small and gnarled, all bent in one direction by the Gulf winds, the oaks on these shell islands always reminded Blacklaws of little old men. And sight of this first *chenière* made him draw rein.

Along this section of the coast there were no shell islands north of Congo Bog. That meant he was already within the limits of the Bog. Blacklaws stared down at the ground, thinking that the man he was following must have known the way, or he wouldn't have taken this route. Yet there was still a reluctance in him. All his life he had heard the stories about this country. About the men who had disappeared within its fastness. About the constant threat of water moccasins and of quicksand that lay on either side of the few trails, ready to suck a man down if he took one step in the wrong direction.

Yet he had the feeling that he was on the trail of something more definite than with what he had been working. A man could read sign and figure things out and use his mind up to a certain point. But there always came a time when he had to take a chance. Blacklaws slackened the reins, touched Tar Baby with a heel, and rode on into the bog.

It was late afternoon, but the twilight filling long stretches of the trail would be there at any time of day, so thick was the canopy of cypress and post oak overhead. It gave the effect of a mauve dream world, smoky and unreal, without enough illumination to cast strong shadow yet filled with lightless pockets that vision would not penetrate. Parrots squawked obscenely from the palmettos. The distant drumming of woodpeckers rarely died. Snakes slithered across the grassed-over trail, spooking his bronc more than once, and herons stamped the glassy waters of swamp pools with their clownish, one-legged reflections.

Day was failing when he came into view of a bayou looping its way southward. It widened here till it reached more than a half a mile from bank to bank, and in its center Blacklaws could see the largest shell island he had come across yet, with the rotting skeleton of a ship's boat sunk into the spit of sand and mud at one end. Chenière Dominique?

He had never seen it before. But its legends were another part of the history of Congo Bog. Jean Lafitte, the

115

pirate of New Orleans, was known to have anchored his ships in the Sabine and to have frequented the country along the river. When Lafitte was captured in 1836, according to the story, his lieutenant, Dominique, had escaped into Congo Bog with the remnants of the pirate crew to establish headquarters there on Chenière Dominique. He had built a house and a cement powder house which was to be used as a fort if they were attacked. There were so many fabulous legends about Lafitte and his lieutenants that Blacklaws had never given the story much attention. Staring at that rotting ship's boat out on the island now, he was filled with an eerie sensation. But something else, too, was in his mind.

Chenière Dominique, Corsica had said. *Could she possibly have known about that rustler*, Blacklaws wondered, *cutting loose from the rest of the rustlers and heading down this way? And, if she did, how could she have known I would be following the rustlers? How could she have known I would pick up his sign or even trail him? And, if she had figured all that out ahead and planted Chenière Dominique in my mind, why? Why would she want me here?*

Again he realized he had reached the point beyond which he could not go in his mind. He had to take the chance, if he wanted to find out. He had lost the tracks of the man within a few yards of the bayou's bank, and he spent a long time studying the ground, without moving into the open or revealing himself to the island, trying to decide whether the horseman had gone directly into the water. It was possible that there were high ridges of shells on the bottom of the bayou that could form trails out to that island. At last, unable to follow the sign into the water, he tied his horse to a cypress and began a careful search up and down the banks for a boat or signs of one. By nightfall he had not come across any. The best he could do was a post oak that had been swept over by the wind to lie with its head in the water, its roots partially torn from the earth. He dug these roots out and finally got the tree shoved off into the water. He took off his boots and used the chin string of his Stetson to tie them together. It was long enough so he could hang them around his neck to dangle down in front of him on either side.

Then he stood there a last moment, a solid silhouette against the texture of evening, his face barely distinguishable with its cheekbones thrusting their blunt edges against the sun-darkened flesh to cast the barest of shadows beneath. Alligators were rumbling down the bayou, and there was an occasional splash out in the inky water. At last he rolled up his pants and waded out to climb aboard the oak. It pitched and rolled with his weight but retained enough spreading branches and rotting foliage to balance the trunk. He bowed forward and began paddling with his hands.

Finally the oaks of the island lifted their twisted silhouettes up before him, and his tree ground against the shells. He pulled his boots on before going ashore and then stepped off. He could not help the crunching of his feet in the deep layer of crushed shells. In a few yards he reached the topsoil that had been blown in to cover the shells, and then he was within the stunted timber.

Once in the trees he moved more cautiously, until at last he reached the clearing. The moon was rising, and its diffused light revealed the legendary stone building, and the sand banked like snowdrifts against its crumbling walls. He stood behind the damp trunk of a post oak, studying the structure. It was not large, perhaps forty feet by twenty, built like a blockhouse with no windows in evidence. The heavy wooden door was still on its hinges, but it was open. There was a hide lying across the threshold. It was covered with the unmistakable mottling of whitish brine, as if it had lain near a place where meat was being salted. It was not a fresh hide. It was stiff and cold. There were no recent signs near the door, either. If signs had been made and then erased, Blacklaws could have told. The only prints were those embedded in the earth, as if a man had stepped through the door while the ground was still wet. But grass grew in these.

Blacklaws got his Remington from its holster and made a careful circle of the building through the trees, without finding anything or any sign. At last, after a half hour of this, he took one step into the open and then wheeled and stepped back to cover. Nothing happened. He stepped out again, this time to cross the open space and stand up against the wall of the building. There were no sounds from within.

He moved around to the door, listening again. There was not enough room in this building to do butchering and pickling in any great numbers. If it was a storeroom, however, he wanted to know. The door was of heavy oak with a rusty latch. It was really only half open, and he had to shove it a little in order to step through. A suffocating warmth filled the interior, laden with the redolence of stagnant water and dank cement. Finally he caught the musty scent of more hides.

He risked a match at last, holding its light cupped in his hands. This vague illumination revealed the room he stood in to be empty except for a wrecked tier of bunks at one side. Pools of moss-edged water covered the cement floor, and spiders scurried from the light. A doorway stood at one end. He walked to this. The portal had fallen from its hinges, and he walked across the rotting boards. It was a smaller, square room. The hides were stacked over to one side. There were only half a dozen, as old and briny as the one outside. Somehow the number did not seem right. If they had cleared it out, would they overlook this many? And if they were still using it, there would be more.

The match burned his fingers. He dropped it and ground it out beneath his heel, turning slowly with the sensation of something wrong. He stepped back through the door, walked across the front room, and was nearly at this door when there came a grunting sound from outside.

He had no clear idea, in that first instant, of what came through the front door. It charged in with a coughing rush, knocking into him so hard he had to stumble backward to keep from falling. Then his foot caught on the rough cement floor, and he was thrown anyway. There was a thudding crash. The dim moonlight was shut off, leaving blackness thick as soot. At the same time a coughing shape crossed above him. Something smashed at his ribs with the beat of a triphammer. Blacklaws fired upward. Then his hand was knocked aside by a second grunting creature that plunged across him.

He rolled over, dazed and shaken. He gained his feet, staggering for the door. Reaching it, he pawed for the handle. He could not find one. Blacklaws faced about, putting his back flat against the door. He knew what had happened now. He was locked inside this building with a pair of wild hogs.

He listened to their chesty grunts, the crackle of their sharp hoofs against the cement floor. Blacklaws knew that, if he had hit either of them, it would be doubly dangerous. Pain and the smell of blood set them off into that wild rage which left nothing in their mind but to rush and gore and kill.

He tried to block his breath off, knowing the slightest sound might betray him. But the struggle had been too violent, and his chest was heaving. The hogs were rooting around through the pools of water across the chamber. One of them ceased its aimless sounds and gave a loud roar. There was that deadly rattle of hoofs.

Blacklaws tried to calculate where it was. He waited till the last instant. Then he fired, jumping aside. The first one smashed into the wall, squealing with pain. But the second one was right behind. It came heavily against Blacklaws and knocked him back against the first floundering razorback.

There was a grunt, a flashing pain in his hand. He no longer held the gun. His hand wet with blood, he threw himself out and away from them. He stumbled, almost fell, and then plunged heavily against the cement of the opposite wall. They wheeled and followed. Again that clatter of hoofs. That grunting roar. He jumped aside, running hard for another wall. He threw himself against this and heard them turn and come after him. He broke back for the wall on the door side. He reached the spot where he had dropped the gun and chanced one instant of going to his knee and pawing about the floor. But he could not find it.

Blacklaws jumped up with a hog coming in from behind. It went past on his left side with a rush. The other one caught him going by his right. Its scaly flank knocked him back onto his knees. Blacklaws was shocked at what an effort it caused him to rise again. He staggered blindly through the darkness to a wall, sagging against it.

He did not know if he had hit either of them when he had fired. And, if he had, he had no way of telling how long they could last with the bullets in them. He had seen many of them fight for ten or fifteen minutes with their bodies riddled. They were circling across the room. One sounded as if it was coughing in pain. Then they seemed to be trotting back his way. One of them gave a triumphant roar and broke toward him. Blacklaws jumped out of the way, but the second hog caught him across the thigh. There was a blow—pain—his feet were carried from the ground with the upward toss of the razorback's head.

He struck the floor, rolled over and over. Coming to a stop in water, he rose, dizzy with pain. There seemed to be walls on either side. And wood. He was in that doorway to the smaller chamber, crouching on the fallen portal. The hogs began at his back again, squealing in their rage. Blacklaws scrambled across the fallen door, going until he came against the wall.

Here he sagged on his knees, drained by the violence of the last few minutes. There was something nagging at his mind. Fresh noises from the other room spun him about. He lost his balance and sprawled across something stiff and hairy. The cowhides in the corner.

Now he knew what had been in his mind. The Indians had used rawhide for shields. He pawed for a handhold, lifting one up. The hogs must have been nosing along the trail of his blood, for they came at a trot. Blacklaws dragged himself up against the wall, holding the iron-tough hide before him. The hogs halted a moment in the doorway, tusks clashing against each other. Then they must have heard the gasping sound of his breath. With a shrill squeal, the first one rushed.

Blacklaws waited till the last instant. Then he jumped aside, holding the hide out like a bullfighter. The hog went into it with a ripping thump. The other animal was right behind, crashing against Blacklaws. He lost his balance and pitched over its body. He rolled over and came onto his hands and knees atop that fallen door. Both hogs wheeled and charged after him. He could hear the bump and clatter of that hide, still hooked onto one razorback's tusk.

Blacklaws plunged through the door, throwing himself aside into the outer room. But the one without the hide sensed this and wheeled after him as it came out the door. It knocked him against the wall. He rolled over and over down the wall to escape its follow-up. It grunted viciously every time it got in close and tossed its head, trying to gore him.

He hit the corner and ran down the other wall until he reached the door again. He could hear that hog out in the middle of the bigger room, bumping and clattering around as it tried to get the hide off its tusk. Blacklaws staggered through the door into the small room and went to his knees at the wall, pawing for another hide.

He got it and was hardly able to rise again. He knew he could not last much longer. The second hog came in through the door after him. Again Blacklaws tried to jump aside with the hide out at his flank. But the hog went against it without hooking a tusk.

It whirled with a wild squeal. He tried to pull the hide back in front of him. The hog came into him with all its weight. There was a sharp rip as one of those tusks went through the hide. It was his thigh that got the point. Blacklaws could not help shouting with the pain. But the hide had kept it from going deep. He pulled free and did not wait for the hog to wrench the hide from his hand.

He jumped over the flapping hide, pawing for the hog. He found a leg, grasped it, pulling the hog off its feet. The beast squealed wildly, still hooked onto that hide. Sharp hoofs sliced at Blacklaws's arms, his belly. He clung to the leg, keeping the beast on its flank, stamping at its head, its ribs, its chest. He kicked savagely, grunting every time he found his mark, till the sounds of the man and beast were indistinguishable.

The hog fought viciously, squealing and coughing. But Blacklaws hung onto that leg, kicking, stamping, till it was the one thing left in his mind. He did not know how long it lasted. He got on his feet and stamped downward. There was the crack of bones and a squeal of pain. Then the hog threw him, and he lay on his side kicking at it. Blacklaws refused to give up that grip on its leg, rolled over to his knees, came up, and began stamping downward again. The hog's struggle threw him again, and he did not have the strength to rise. He lay there kicking at it till he could not even kick any more. All he could do was hang onto that leg.

The hog's efforts were feeble, too, now. Its leg twitched weakly in his hands. Its sounds were shallow and pain ridden. Blacklaws let go and crawled away on his belly until he was against the wall. He could not move any farther. If the hog was going to kill him now, he couldn't help it. He was drained of vitality and of will. But the hog did not move. Its grunts died down. Dimly, Blacklaws tried to hear the other hog. There was no sound in the next room. He finally realized it was the other hog he had hit with his shots, and they had finally killed it.

He was still lying there, half conscious, when there was a noise outside. The door opened. He could not react in any way. He could not move. He simply lay there, staring at the moonlit rectangle made by the open door. Then the silhouette of a man moved into it.

Chapter Thirteen

Quintin Garland hated the bayou country at night. The sounds were hateful, and the smells were hateful, and the land itself was hateful. It seemed the rumbling of the alligators would never stop. The fog rolled up off the

water like steam reeking of rotten bottom mud and dead
fish. Streamers of moss were constantly trailing their
clammy cerements across Garland's face. He brushed
them off with a curse and reined his Copperbottom
against Phil's nag to grab the boy's arm.

"How much farther now, Phil? We must be nearly to
the coast. Seems like we've been riding all night."

Phil lay forward across the saddle horn, barely able
to hold himself on the horse. His head rolled upward
with great effort. His face had a sallow hue in this darkness, and he had trouble focusing his glazed eyes. Garland felt a frustrated anger as he saw the delirium in
those eyes. The boy had been unconscious all that first
night in the cabin and then delirious the next day and
night. Garland had been unable to get anything coherent
from him till the second morning, when Phil seemed to
be somewhat lucid and had started giving directions.
They had been traveling since noon now, forced to stop
once for three hours when Phil passed out. Garland
shook him again.

"Phil?"

"This is the fork," mumbled Phil. "Take the one on
the right, Dee."

"It isn't Dee, you fool . . . ," Garland broke off impatiently, gigging his horse forward, taking the turnoff.

Hibiscus mottled the darkness in chalk-white patches,
sometimes lending such a luminous glow in the fog that
Phil's tired mare spooked at its ghostly apparition. It was
a narrower trail, overgrown with bindweed, showing little use. This puzzled Garland. It should show a lot of
use. They couldn't drag that many hides in here without . . . ! They broke suddenly into a clearing on a bank
of the bayou. There was a shack here, built of mud-
blackened cypress logs, its saddle roof sagging in the
middle.

Garland wheeled to the boy. "Where are we?"

"Mock's," said Phil weakly.

"Mock's! Phil, what did you bring us here for? This isn't the place. You know that!"

"I can't go any farther. Please. . . ."

Phil's voice faded out, and he slacked off to slide softly from his horse to the ground. Garland dismounted and walked around to where Phil lay, dropping on one knee beside him.

"Damn you, Phil. You know I didn't mean here. You never meant to keep your word. . . ."

Garland broke off sharply. Perhaps some lifting movement of his horse's head had warned him. He turned to see a man standing at the corner of the shack, a dim silhouette in the fog, slop-gutted and bowlegged. It was Mock Fannin. He came over to them without speaking and hunkered down beside Garland, staring at Phil.

"Phil's been shot. What the hell did you bring him clear out here for?" Mock broke off, to look up at Garland. "What kind of trouble's he in?" he asked at last.

"I don't know," Garland said. "He just came to my place and asked for help. I figured the first place they'd look for him was his house."

Mock slipped his hands under Phil's arms. "Get his feet. Help me in with him."

Reluctantly, Garland went to Phil's feet. The boy was dead weight and a great labor to get into the shack. There was only one large room, stinking of rotten mud and fried fish and cheap whiskey. The hog-fat candle flickering on the table cast an uncertain light out into the chamber, leaving its corners and the bunks at either wall pocketed in black shadows. It was not till Garland had lowered Phil onto the bunk which Mock indicated, and straightened up, that he saw the man in the other bunk. The name left him in a surprised whisper.

"Kenny?"

Blacklaws rolled up onto one elbow, staring silently

at Garland. In the gloom over there the heavy strength of his face shaped up dimly, the eyes deeply recessed in hollows of shadow. The blanket covered him to the knees. Below this the legs of his pants were ripped and torn and grimed with a white substance that gleamed like brine in the light, except at the edges of each tear, where a crust of dried blood made a coppery stain. Garland moved forward, hardly realizing he was doing so, until he reached the table.

"What happened?" he asked.

"Big card game," Mock said. "Big card game fight. Kenny killed seventeen men."

"That white stuff looks like you've been on the shell islands," said Garland.

"Does it?" asked Blacklaws.

Garland's hands flattened out on the table top. "How did you get so ripped up?"

"Big knife fight," Mock said.

"Looks more like you got in a nest of wild hogs," Garland said, bending forward intensely. "Is that what happened, Kenny? Did some hogs attack you?"

"Card game. Seventeen men."

"Shut up, Mock," snapped Garland. Something was eating at him now. Tate had tried to kill Blacklaws. That was obvious. How else would Blacklaws get mixed up with hogs? But somehow that wasn't the question in Garland's mind.

"We passed a lot of shell islands coming in," he said. "We even saw Chenière Dominique. It was the only one big enough for something like this to happen. What were you doing on Chenière Dominique, Kenny?"

"Take it easy, Quintin," Mock said. "Kenny's a sick man."

But Garland found himself staring fixedly at Blacklaws. How had Tate lured Blacklaws to the island? Only one thing was big enough to decoy him out here. The

hide factory. Tate had been right. Blacklaws was working for Carew.

"Kenny,"—Garland's lips shaped the words stiffly—
"what were you doing on Chenière Dominique?"

"Just riding, Quintin."

"You weren't." Garland found himself moving
around the table. "You weren't just riding. What were
you doing . . . ?"

Garland quit moving then and talking. Some new expression had come into Blacklaws's face. Pain and
weakness seemed to leave him more withdrawn than
ever, but the expression on his face still had changed.
Garland could not keep from swinging his glance around
to Mock. There was a sly knowledge in the man's dissolute eyes.

"Didn't know Dominique's island meant that much
to you, Quintin," he grinned blandly.

Garland felt his weight settle. What a fool he was!
Why had he let them see how much that meant to him?
Why did he always lose his head where Blacklaws was
concerned?

Still grinning, Mock began unwinding the blood-
soaked bandage Garland had put on Phil's wound. He
stopped half way through, raising his head. Garland
heard it then. The soft slap-slap of a paddle out in the
bayou. Mock shuffled to the candle and snuffed it out.
In the darkness Garland heard the man move to the door
and open it. The catwalk of split Davy Crockett logs ran
down across the rotten bottom mud to a makeshift jetty
of post-oak stumps and the sideboards and strakes of an
old skiff. Drawn up against this jetty were two pirogues—the canoe of the bayou country—made from
hollowed logs tapered at each end. Fog was so thick that
the end of the jetty was hardly visible, and the river
beyond was swallowed in a milky mist.

The third pirogue seemed to swim out of this, coming

toward the jetty. A ghostly craft, at first, with two tenebrous figures in it. Garland was at the door by the time the pirogue thudded softly into the jetty. One of the figures swung out onto the platform in a cat-like movement to help the other out. The catwalk swayed and clattered with their movement toward the shack. They seemed to float in out of the fog. Only a few feet from the door they were still merely diffused shapes. The height, the immense shoulders of the taller figure, stamped it as being Rouquette. The other looked like a woman in some kind of heavy cloak.

"I don't see a light," she said.

"I'm here, Corsica," Mock said. "Just snuffed out the candle."

"Mock." It came in a little gasp. "You startled me."

"I'll light up," Mock answered.

Garland stepped aside as the man turned for the table. Corsica and the giant Os Rouge waited till the candlelight spread out from the table, lapping at their feet. The cape over Corsica's riding habit was a deep wine color, losing its redness in this poor light till it was almost as black as her hair. Rouquette was barefoot and wore no more than greasy rawhide *chivarras* for pants. His inevitable grin made a bone-white flash beneath the prominent knobs of Indian cheekbones. Surprise parted Corsica's lips with her first sight of Garland.

"Quintin, what are you doing here?"

"I might ask you the same thing."

"You're not in court now, so can't you answer a simple question?" she said impatiently. "I'm looking for Phil. He's been gone three days now. I made Rouquette bring me down here. I thought Mock might know something."

"You'd better come in, Corsica."

The strange tone of Mock's voice lifted her chin. Then she came in past Garland, with Rouquette moving behind, and halted sharply. The shadows obscured Black-laws, as they had when Garland first came in, and Corsica saw Phil first. She remained there an instant, staring at him with a face drained of color and then rushed over to drop on her knees beside him.

"What is it? He's shot? What is it, Mock?"

"Garland can tell you," Mock said.

She wheeled, still on her knees. Before she could speak to Garland, however, the corner of her vision picked up the dim figure on the other bunk. Garland saw the same flutter come to her eyes as must have come to his, with their effort to adjust to the shadows beyond the candlelight.

"Kenny."

It was hardly a whisper from her. He lay on his side, staring at her without offering to speak. His pants were still visible below the blanket, covered with that white residue of crushed shells and that copper-black stain about the long rips. A scar lay like an ugly stripe down the length of one cheek.

"Looks like the hogs have been at that one, Miss Corsica," grinned Rouquette.

"Hogs? Where?"

"Chenière Dominique."

It left Garland in a bitter accusation, before he could stop himself, and afterward he was sorry. Corsica sent him a sharply puzzled glance, speaking to Blacklaws.

"Phil was there with you?"

"No," Blacklaws said wearily. "Phil wasn't there."

Still on her knees she turned back to her brother, fright shining in her eyes. "Then what . . . ?"

"It won't be fatal, Corsica," said Mock. "His injuries are swollen, and he has fever, but I think he'll be all right."

She stared at Phil a moment longer, biting her under-lip. Then she swung wide and luminous eyes up to Garland. She did not speak. No one spoke. He knew they were waiting. His boots made an angry scrape against the floor.

"Phil came to my place this way," he said. "In some kind of trouble."

"*Your* place." Corsica was incredulous. "And you brought him way down here . . . in this shape?"

"I thought it would be dangerous to take him home."

"Dangerous? As dangerous as bringing him down here? Through the night, the rain . . . ?"

"Now, don't go misjudging Garland," Mock told her. "It was purely out of the goodness of his heart."

She continued to stare up at Garland, her eyes narrowing till he could barely see them behind the lids. "What did you hope to gain by bringing him down here, Quintin?"

"Gain?" He felt the heated flush rise in his face. "I stood to gain nothing, Corsica. In fact, I stood to lose everything, if it were found out I aided a criminal to escape. I didn't want to say it that way, Corsica. But if you refuse to see it, I probably saved your brother's life, and you accuse me of doing it for some kind of selfish purpose."

There was a silence. Corsica's face had sharpened under the sting of Garland's words, and there was a relenting in her eyes. Then Mock chuckled.

"Garland was mighty curious about why Kenny was on Chenière Dominique," he said. "Do you really think there's a hide factory on that island, Rouquette?"

Surprise robbed Rouquette's gleaming face of that broad smile, but before he could answer, Corsica glanced swiftly at Mock. "Hide factory? Why should there be a . . . ?" She broke off, looking back at Garland. "Is that what kind of trouble Phil was in? Had he been rustling some hides?"

"How do I know?" asked Garland.

"I think you do." That relenting expression was gone from her face. "You thought Phil had been rustling hides. You thought he knew where the hidden packery is located. Is that what Mock meant? You want to know where the packery is too? You deliberately used Phil's condition to force it from him. You made him bring you all the way out here, in that shape . . . !"

Her voice had risen higher with each word to break off suddenly. She stared wide-eyed at him for another moment. Then she turned away, her hands clenched at her sides.

"Corsica. . . ."

"Don't speak to me, Quintin," she said.

There was another strained silence. Rouquette's bare feet shuffled on the puncheon floor. Corsica turned to Mock, speaking in a brittle voice.

"I'm staying here with Phil."

"You'd better not, Corsica," Mock told her. "The sheriff will be coming around to your place. I'm surprised he hasn't come already. If you're gone when he comes, it will really put a bee in his bonnet."

She shook her head from side to side, frowning. "Then we can take Phil back now."

"You know you can't. He's already had too much punishment."

She stood there for a long moment, staring at Mock. Garland saw defeat settle into her face. She turned back to her brother. "Phil," she said in a small voice, "why . . . ?" She broke off helplessly. She turned to look at Blacklaws. Her lips parted, as if she meant to speak. Nothing came out.

"Kenny'll be all right too, Corsica," grinned Mock. "You just leave it up to old Doc Fannin."

"Will you need anything?" she asked dully.

"Whiskey." Mock licked his lips. "Lots of that. Big

medicinal value. Cure anything. Clean clothes for both of them. Coffee, if you can get it.''

She nodded dumbly—still staring at Blacklaws. There was something between them in that moment that Garland couldn't read. Blacklaws's face was bleak and withdrawn. Some small reaction to the expression of his eyes ran through Corsica's face. She held out her hand, a deep compassion showed in her parted lips.

''Kenny,'' she said.

His answer was barely audible. ''What?''

There was a long pause. She dropped the hand helplessly. ''I'm sorry,'' she murmured.

''Don't be,'' Blacklaws whispered. ''*I'll* never be sorry.''

Mock shuffled forward, taking her arm. ''Come on, now. The quicker you get back the better. They'll be all right.''

She turned her eyes to Garland for an instant, as she passed. They flashed like a naked blade in the light. Then that was gone, and she was past him. Mock dropped her arm when she reached the door, and she stepped outside alone. Rouquette started to follow, but Mock caught his arm. Garland saw his chance and went by them after Corsica. Behind, Mock began saying something to Rouquette in a low voice. Garland caught up with Corsica half way down the plank walk.

''Corsica,'' he said, ''you can't think I'd be capable of . . . ?''

''I don't know what you'd be capable of, Quintin,'' she said, wheeling to look up at him with those accusing eyes. ''A month ago, two months, I would have thought you were doing it for Phil's sake. Now . . . ?''

''Now what, Corsica?'' he asked, bending toward her.

Her shoulders sagged. ''I asked you to make me stay proud of you, Quintin. You haven't tried very hard.''

''Blacklaws put this in your mind. Mock and Blacklaws. You can't believe their insidious . . . !''

"No, Quintin," she said tiredly, "whatever there is in my mind was put there by what *you did*, not by what they said. Now let me go. I don't want to talk about it any more."

"Corsica. . . ."

"Let me go," she said sharply and tore loose to turn and half run down the puncheon walk. Then the walk began to shake with a heavier weight, and Garland swung around barely in time to allow Rouquette past. There was no misinterpreting the brazen grin on the man's varnished face.

" 'Evening, Mister Garland."

Garland watched him go, watched him help Corsica into the pirogue and get in himself, turning the boat out into the fog. Then Garland went back up the catwalk. There was something goading about Mock Fannin's primitive silhouette in the doorway. Without speaking to him, Garland left the catwalk and went to his horse. He mounted absently and took up the lead rope of the other animal, gigging his horse out onto the trail.

Somehow the only thing in his mind was Blacklaws. Garland's whole defeat here seemed to revolve around the man. It had started when Garland revealed how much he wanted to know what Blacklaws was doing on Chenière Dominique. He wouldn't have given himself away but for Blacklaws. And Mock wouldn't have guessed his desire to know where the hidden packery was, wouldn't have tied it up to Phil, and put it in Corsica's mind that Garland had used Phil for that reason.

He hadn't risked the boy's life, Garland told himself. *He had saved it. Why couldn't she see that? Because of Blacklaws. Everything was because of Blacklaws. And that expression on her face when she had taken that last look at the man. Garland hadn't missed it. That interchange about being sorry and not being sorry—was*

Kenny coming between them in that way too? They'd had opportunity to be alone together.

Garland now felt a hate rising so strongly it almost gagged him. *He couldn't let Blacklaws do that to him. Corsica couldn't have any real feelings for the man. She was probably just mixed up. If it wasn't for the way Blacklaws had spoken, he could believe he had raped Corsica. As it was, he might well have seduced her in a weak moment. Well, if he had or hadn't, he would pay for turning Corsica against him.*

The packery! Above all, there was the packery. He couldn't let Blacklaws find the packery before he did. It would ruin everything.

The idea forming in Garland's mind was not completely new. He had considered getting Blacklaws out of the way before. Blacklaws was at Mock's recovering because he had arranged for Tate to finish him, and Tate had bungled the job. Before this Garland had never actually considered removing Blacklaws himself. Now there could be no more indirection about it. He would do it himself.

Chapter Fourteen

After they had left, Blacklaws lay motionless on the bunk. He was still too sick, too weak from his battle to think very clearly. He was hot from the fever. The wounds Mock had treated and bound up throbbed insistently. His mind worked turgidly with his thoughts of

Corsica. *Had she really driven him out to that shell island? He didn't want to believe it. Had she known Tate was planning something like that? Or had she put him up to it?* He tossed feebly. He didn't want to think about it. He was too sick even to think about it.

"Sure held up supper," muttered Mock, shuffling around the room. "Soon's I fix Phil, I'll get us some food. How about some bowfin tonight, Kenny?" He glanced over at Blacklaws and grinned. "Don't look like that. They're good as catfish if you cook them right. Most people make 'em taste like wet cotton. Got to soak 'em overnight in vinegar and oil. Better'n chicken."

He was hunting through a shelf for some clean cloth for Phil's bandage. "Funny thing about those bowfin. The way their swim bladder's put in, they can breathe air and live in mud. I've seen them plowed alive out of a field weeks after high water's backed down. The one I got here, now. Had to climb a tree for him. Last flood must have left him there. He'd built himself a nest and started laying woodpecker eggs."

Blacklaws did not answer, and Mock puttered around making a poultice of lard and gun powder for Phil's wounds. It was an old remedy, and it drew like fire, but Blacklaws had seen it work wonders with an infected wound.

"See them seventeen new locks on the door?" Mock asked.

Blacklaws' eyes swung to the door. Then they closed, as he realized what Mock meant. It was starting, then. He wondered if he was too weak to fool Mock. Or maybe Mock had guessed the whole thing.

"If you're talking about that latch on the door at Chenière Dominique, it wasn't new," Blacklaws said.

"I thought it was funny there should be any locks on the door," Mock said. "Last time I was there, it didn't have any. I scraped at one. Things rust pretty fast out

135

here, Kenny. Leave something out overnight, and you got a layer of rust. Rub it in the mud and it'll look pretty old. It was nice and shiny and new underneath, though.''

"So Tate put an iron latch on the door," Blacklaws said dully. "He couldn't have made a wooden one that would have held very well with that cement wall."

"Where do you suppose he'd get seventeen locks, Kenny?"

"Deller's store, I suppose. Only place around here."

"Tate wouldn't have money for it. He's never had a cent."

"Maybe he traded Deller a shoat for it."

"Deller won't deal with him. Tate's tried it before."

"You're thinking somebody else got it for Tate?" asked Blacklaws. When Mock did not answer, Blacklaws turned to see him grinning slyly. Blacklaws tossed restlessly. "Maybe you're on the wrong track, Mock. I checked for fresh sign before I went in that powder house. The place hadn't been entered in months. . . ." He broke off, realizing how much he had revealed.

Mock was opening cartridges and emptying the black powder into a plate. He began to mix lard with this. "Tate could drive a herd of cattle through your front yard and never leave a trace," he murmured.

"You haven't told me how you got on Chenière Dominique," Blacklaws said.

"I was fishing near the island," Mock told him. "Heard the shot. It must have been the one you let go before Tate slammed the door. I went to have a look-see." He raised his eyes, filled with that dissolute wisdom and with what had been on his mind. "So you checked for fresh sign. Like you always do, Kenny? Or was it something special?"

Blacklaws licked dry lips. "Corsica came to me yesterday about Phil. He'd been gone a day then. The least I could do was take a look. I found sign of the hide rustlers, found where one man had broken away. Cold trail, but it led me down into Congo Bog.''

''You figure Tate planted the whole thing?''

''No. I think one of the rustlers really did turn off and go as far south as Bayou Lafitte. He went into the bayou just north of Congo Bog. It looked like he forded and came out on the other side, but I got the feeling something was wrong. Nothing I could put my finger on. The prints looked the same and were sure enough a couple of days old. Still, I had the feeling something was wrong.''

''You think Tate took it up there?'' asked Mock.

''I think the rustler stayed in the water, turning upstream or down to hide his tracks. Tate made the tracks on the other side, so it looked like the man I'd trailed came out on the opposite bank and went on into Congo Bog.''

''How could Tate shave it so close?'' asked Mock. ''Surely he'd know you could tell the difference between the two sets of tracks.''

''That's the point. There wasn't a difference. The only way he could have done that was to know who the rustler was and steal his horse for that night.''

Mock shook his head, snorting. ''I wouldn't put it beyond that crazy hog toller. Then you figure Tate waited on the island for you?''

''Or on the bank and pushed off in a boat with those hogs after he saw me go across,'' Blacklaws said.

''But how would he know you'd be trailing that hide rustler in the first place?'' Mock said.

''Probably knew Phil was in trouble and that I'd be hunting him,'' Blacklaws said.

Mock looked up from kneading the poultice, his hands grimy with lard and gun powder. ''Or knew you was hunting the hidden packery and could be led onto Chenière Dominique if you thought the packery was there?''

The silence after that seemed to press heavily against Blacklaws's chest till he found it difficult to breathe. He hadn't wanted to face it like this. He had known it would come sooner or later, but he hadn't wanted to face it.

"Is that what you think, Mock?" he said at last.

Mock dropped his eyes uncomfortably to the table. "Why not look square at it, Kenny? What do you think?"

Blacklaws rolled his head restlessly. "I guess you know."

"You was wondering whether Phil brought Garland here just because I was a cousin of the Manattes or because I was in the hide rustling with him."

Blacklaws stared at the ceiling without answering. Mock looked down at his glistening hands.

"Sometimes I wish you hadn't come back, Kenny," he said at last.

Blacklaws had nightmares later on. Nightmares of giant hogs swarming all over him, their mouths gaping, their tusks setting up an unholy clatter. He did not know how many times he awoke with Mock holding him down and trying to soothe him. The fever was still with him the second day, and he lay in a semi-stupor, perspiring heavily with pain and weakness. Phil was more violent, thrashing about wildly and calling Corsica or babbling about Garland. He quieted in the afternoon, however, and Mock asked Blacklaws if it would be all right to leave them alone an hour or so. He had to go fishing if they were to have anything for supper. Blacklaws told him to go ahead then settled back to try and nap. Afternoon waned slowly, with the sun coming around and shining obliquely through the doorway, adding its brazen heat to the suffocating humidity already filling the shack. Blacklaws threw off the cover, drenching the straw tick with his sweat.

"Garland, that's a damn fool idea. You'll never get anywhere with that!"

Phil screamed it like a woman in pain and began thrashing in his bunk again. It lifted Blacklaws up in startled surprise. The pain of his wounds caught him, and he sagged back. But Phil continued to thrash around so wildly that Blacklaws was afraid he would throw himself out of the bunk. Finally Blacklaws tried to get up again and go over to the delirious boy.

He got his feet swung to the floor and almost pitched over on his face when he tried to rise. He was surprised at how weak he was. He could not make it standing up and went to hands and knees. Half way across the room everything started spinning, and he clutched at a chair to keep himself from toppling over. At first he thought he was going to pass out. Then he thought he would be sick. Finally the nausea passed. Phil was still screaming and laughing, and Blacklaws forced himself to crawl over to him across the floor. He reached the bunk on hands and knees and hung there on the sideboard, panting feebly, trying to gather his strength.

"Take it easy, Phil," he gasped. "You're not with Garland now. You're at Mock's. You're safe."

"Garland!" Phil heaved up, laughing wildly again. "Brand them through a blanket, Quintin? You're crazy."

Blacklaws stopped trying to calm him, frowning. "Who brands through a blanket?"

"Everybody," raved Phil. "Take a wet blanket. Take a Bar T brand. You can change it into a Curry Comb by running a couple more new bars on top. If you do the whole thing through a wet blanket and run your iron over the old scars too, it'll make them look fresh as the new ones. I seen a man do it once . . . fresh as the new ones. You're crazy, Quintin, you'll never get that on Roman. I've been down to his place when he's skinning.

Only brand that shows through to the inside is his Double Sickle.''

"Phil . . . !'' Blacklaws caught at him, forgetting his own pain now, realizing he was on the trail of something. "What if something else did burn through?''

"Roman wouldn't be that big a fool.'' Phil thrashed over against the wall. "Even in the early days he wouldn't. It'd be too obvious how they changed a Quarter Moon to a Double Sickle''

"Take it easy, Phil. Lie down and relax. Garland's gone,'' Blacklaws said. He rubbed his hand up and down Phil's arm and went on talking to him in that crooning voice. It had the same quieting effect as it did on his horse, when she was spooked. Finally Phil lay back, gave up, and fell into a fretful sleep.

But now Blacklaws was putting it together and realizing what it meant. Roman had grown big fast during the war. There had always been vague rumors that he was not above rustling to gain his ends. But there had never been proof, and the stories were usually circulated by his enemies. The wet-blanket technique had been popular at that time, tracing a new brand over an old one through the blanket so that the old scars looked as fresh as the new. But sometimes the first brand had been put on a thin patch of hide and had burned to the inside, whereas the mark made through the blanket might not burn clear through the hide. That left the original brand showing on the inside of the hide. A cow had to be skinned to prove it. But they were skinning them by the thousands now.

So that's what Garland's found, Blacklaws thought. *He's come across a hide somewhere that proves Roman was a wet-blanket artist. Phil said the Quarter Moon? It would have to be an old steer. The Quarter Moon went out of business ten years ago. An old steer with the Double Sickle put on over the original Quarter Moon*

*but with that Quarter Moon showing up on the inside of
the hide. It's good, Quintin,* he thought. *It's good.*

*And what could that mean to Roman? It would be
positive proof of his earlier rustling. The other members
of the Jefferson Association wouldn't stand for it. He'd
be ruined if not jailed. Roman wouldn't touch the hide
rustlers if they held that over his head.*

Blacklaws raised his eyes as the catwalk began shaking outside. Mock came in, breathing heavily.

"Phil got delirious again," Blacklaws told him.

Mock did not seem to hear that.

"Listen," he said, "the sheriff's right on the edge of
Congo Bog with the whole Seventeenth Cavalry. I saw
him. They're headed in here. I think I'd better get Phil
some place. Think you can manage it alone for a day?"

"I'll be all right. Where will you take him?"

"Back to the Manatte house is the only thing I know.
I don't think anybody in town knows about that old
storm cellar where the slave cabins used to be."

"I wish I could help you get him out."

"You'd better stay here," Mock said. "They aren't
after you."

He helped Blacklaws back to his bunk. Then he pulled
his Thuers conversion from its holster, handing it to him.

"This is the best I can do, Kenny. I'll take that old
Henry repeater for myself. I'll stop at Chenièrc Dominique on my way back and try to pick up your horse
and your gun."

Blacklaws checked the loads on the six-shooter, slid
it under his pillow.

"Thanks, Mock," he said.

Mock got some blankets wrapped around Phil and
then bent to help him out of the bunk. Phil began thrashing, but Mock finally got him on his feet. They staggered
out of the shack like a pair of drunks, with Phil raving
about how the saddle horn kept hurting his chest. They

almost spilled off the catwalk several times before they reached the boat. It was a battle to get Phil in the pirogue. Mock straightened up then, turning to look back through the open door.

"War bag all laced up, Kenny?"

"All laced up, Mock."

Mock stared a moment longer, and Blacklaws wondered what he was thinking. Then he turned to drop in the pirogue and shove off. The narrow boat disappeared around a shaggy turn, and Blacklaws lowered his head back onto the pillow, turning it so he could still see through the door.

The sun was low in the west, sending a flood of crimson light directly in the open door to lend the room and its meager furnishings a macabre, bloody tint. A pair of alligators pulled up on the mud flats across the bayou, grunting heavily. All the late afternoon sounds were drowsy and muffled. The raucous call of mallards, stippling the sky with their wedge as they swung coastward. The cackling of turkeys in some distant bottom. The rustle of small animals in the tangled thickets about the shack. The warmth and the peace of it made Blacklaws realize that spring was not far off. It filled him with a sense of well being despite the dull throbbing of his wounds, and presently he went to sleep.

When he awoke, the sun was gone. The mallards were no longer in sight. Twilight saturated the land with a copper stain. A wind had risen, whipping the bayou into choppy crosscurrents. It caught up a scrap of paper in the room and rattled it across the floor to come up against the bunk. Blacklaws felt cold and rolled over. A wave of nausea swept him, and he hung his head over the side, waiting for that to pass. When he finally raised his head again, Gauche Sallier stood in the doorway.

The two of them stared at each other without speaking

for what seemed a long time. Finally, though the Creole was in silhouette, his teeth made a chalky flash against the dark enigma of his face.

"Good evening, *m'sieu.*"

"You looking for Mock?" Blacklaws asked.

"Are you sick, *m'sieu?*"

"No."

Sallier came through the door. Agate Ayers appeared behind him and came in too. He looked at Blacklaws's torn clothes. He rubbed at his little potbelly meditatively.

"Looks like you've been in a fight," he said.

"What's on your mind?" Blacklaws asked.

"Phil Manatte."

"I don't know where he is."

"He isn't home, for sure," Agate said. "The sheriff was there today."

"What are you hunting him for?"

"Don't you know, *m'sieu?*"

"No."

"Sheriff Sheridan would like him."

"Are you with the sheriff?"

"You don't know where Phil is?"

"I told you."

"You look bad off," Agate said.

"Not bad."

"Can you get up?"

"If I want."

"Can you now?" Sallier caught up one of the hide-bottomed chairs from the table, swinging it around beside the bunk, and lowering himself in it. Then he leaned forward and lifted his hand. Blacklaws could not stop the stiffening of his body. This brought a sardonic smile to Sallier's face. He merely pointed to the wound on Blacklaws's arm.

"Is that the worst one?" he asked.

"None of them is bad."

143

"*Non*?" Sallier put his hand against Blacklaws's bandaged stomach and pushed. Blacklaws could not help the hoarse grunt of pain that left him. He lunged back against the wall to escape the pressure.

"Ain't that a sack of hell?" said Agate.

"I want to know where Phil Manatte is, *m'sieu*."

"I don't know, I told you. . . ."

"Don't you?"

Sallier reached out again. Blacklaws grabbed his hand. Sallier put pressure on. Blacklaws was too weak to keep the hand from moving in. He released Sallier and lunged for the Thuers. He got the pillow torn off and the gun in his hand before Agate reached him. The man caught his wrist and swept his hand against the wall so hard the gun leaped out of his fingers and off the edge of the bed onto the floor. Agate scooped it off the floor and put it on the table.

"I thought so," he said. "Now ask him where Phil is."

Blacklaws lay huddled over on his side, eyes squinted with the pain of his smashed hand. "I don't know," he said.

"He seems very weak, Agate. Perhaps you can hold him."

Agate came around the chair and bent into the bunk. Blacklaws tried to fend him off. Agate caught one of his wrists and gave a heave that pulled Blacklaws flat on his belly. Agate caught the other wrist and twisted Blacklaws over onto his back. Then he pinned both wrists against the sweat-drenched tick. Blacklaws writhed feebly for a moment. Then he stopped. The Creole was looking at his leg.

"This one looks even worse than the stomach, Agate."

"Try it."

Sallier reached down to spread the torn edges of cloth

carefully apart. He began to smile again. He probed through the bandage with his forefinger. He found the hole and dug deeply. The breath came out of Blacklaws in a hoarse gust.

"Where is Phil, *m'sieu*?"

"I don't know."

"Dig deeper, Gauche."

"Where is Phil, *m'sieu*?"

"Damn you, I don't know, I told you."

"Where is Phil?"

"Goddamn you, Sallier."

"Where, *m'sieu*?"

Suddenly a roar broke through all the shouting and thrashing. Sallier's hand was torn away from Blacklaws's leg. There was a crackling scrape of chair legs across the floor. Blacklaws opened his eyes to see John Roman dragging the chair backward with Sallier still in it. Roman had simply grabbed its back with one hand and hauled away from the bunk in a great arc. It upset as it smashed into the table and spilled the Creole out onto the floor. At the same time Agate released Blacklaws's wrists and wheeled toward Roman. But he was too late.

Letting go of the chair, Roman reached Agate before he could move, smashing him brutally in the face. It knocked him back into the wall so hard the whole building shook. Sallier was rolling over and going for his gun. Roman jumped back at him and kicked it out of his hand. Then he kicked him in the face, knocking him back under the table. After that Roman stood panting in the middle of the room.

"Of all the damn' snakes I ever saw," he said. "I ought to skin you and render your lard like a steer. Don't have enough guts to stand up against a whole man, two of you on one at that ... !"

He trailed off into a raging wheeze, as if unable to

express himself adequately. Agate stood pinned against the wall, gaping at him. There was more anger in Sallier as he crawled from beneath the table, holding his bloody face. He got to his feet and stood there, trembling. When his voice finally came, it had a hissing, womanish tone.

"You told us to find out where Phil was."

"Not that way," Roman told him. "Not torturin' a sick man. I ought to kick your face in again." He turned and stepped over to Blacklaws. "What'd they do, Kenny?"

Blacklaws lay heavily in the bed, only feebly holding back the pain so his cheeks were drawn in till the blunt edges of his strong cheekbones shone dully through the flesh. "No permanent damage, Roman," he said, staring half lidded up at the man. Suddenly his lips spread in a weak grin. "You're getting soft," he said.

Roman snorted. "Don't make that mistake, Kenny. If I wanted anything from you when you were healthy, I'd gladly beat it out myself. But nobody'll ever say John Roman kicked a man while he was down." He half turned to Agate. "I've got a pint of whiskey in my sougan. Get it for me." Then he wheeled on around to wave an arm at the Creole. "You get out too, you damn' snake, get out and wait for me."

Sallier had wiped his face clean of blood with his neckerchief. He went over to pick his gun up off the floor and stood there, holding it a minute, eyes smoldering. Roman faced him without a sound. Agate passed across in front of Sallier and out the door.

Finally Sallier said: "Someday, John, somebody is going to kill you."

"He'll have to have more guts than you," Roman said. "Put that gun away and get out."

Sallier continued to stare at him. Then he put the gun back and turned to walk out the door. Roman glanced toward Blacklaws.

"They thought you knew where Phil was?" he asked.

"What made you think Phil would be here?" Black-laws asked.

"He ain't at home. Mock's the next bet." Roman bent toward Blacklaws. "Do you know where he is, Kenny?"

"No."

Agate came in with the whiskey. Roman went to the shelves and got a tin cup. With one hand he dragged the table over next to the bunk and set cup and bottle down on it. Then he poured half a cupful for Blacklaws and held his head up for a drink. Blacklaws squinted his eyes shut, as the raw fire of it spread out through him and then lay back, licking his lips.

"What put you in this fix?" Roman asked at last.

Blacklaws did not answer at first. Then a smile fluttered one end of his mouth and died away. "Big card game," he said soberly. "Big card game fight. I killed seventeen men."

Roman frowned sharply, started to speak. He checked himself, eyes narrowing till they were hardly visible in their whiskey-veined pouches, as he stared down at Blacklaws. Finally he dismissed it with an angry snort.

"I'll leave the bottle here where you can get it," he said.

"Should I thank you?"

"I'll take it out of your hide when you're well."

Blacklaws's eyes were still closed, but he was grinning again. "That's what I like to hear, John," he murmured.

He heard Agate go out again, heard the puncheon flooring tremble beneath Roman's weight. Then the stabbing tattoo of the man's footsteps ceased. Blacklaws lifted his lids to see Roman standing in the doorway. He made a broad, barrel-shaped silhouette, against the last light of day. One hand was against the door frame, and he had turned to look back at Blacklaws, his chin sunk

147

deeply into his neck. That sullen expression was barely visible in the shadowy creases of his face.

"Wipe the smile off," he said. "You won't have any reason for it the next time we meet."

Chapter Fifteen

Spring was bursting the land now. Huisache was a prodigal Midas, flinging its golden bloom through the thicket. The fresh-fallen snowdrifts of daisies lined the roads and the tufted tips of buffalo clover bobbed on windy ridges like a host of cottontails. The honk of migrating geese constantly heralded the new season, and the sky over Copper Bluffs was never empty of their northward-flying wedges.

Quintin Garland felt none of the rebirth swelling the land. He spent most of his time in the office now, on the second floor of the French House. He had few clients left, and nobody had been to see him during the ten days since he had taken Phil to Mock's. That did not bother him so much as the fact that the rustlers had still not gotten in touch with him. Surely the word of his offer had reached them by now. If Tate had not carried it, one of the other brushpoppers he had told would sooner or later get it through. It was his last chance. There was money in what they were doing. There would be more money in it, with what he had to hold over Roman's head. He could smash Roman with it, and that would be tantamount to smashing the Jefferson Cattle Association itself, for Roman was the only man who really held it together.

Perhaps Garland could have ruined Roman as completely by turning his evidence of Roman's earlier rustling over to the law, but that would profit him little. It might gain him some small recognition, might restore the faith of the town in him. Yet, what could that lead to? Nothing but the resumption of the same stupid, penny-pinching routine of being a small-town lawyer. That was not for him. He had seen too many men waste their lives struggling to rise that way.

He had never stopped to analyze or question the ambition which gnawed at him so insistently. Perhaps part of it had been inherited from his father. Martin Garland had been noted for his ambition. Perhaps another part had come from the intense poverty of Quintin's youth. He never regretted this desire to achieve. In the few times he had stopped to look at it objectively, he welcomed it. Without ambition, what was a man? A drunken brushpopper like Mock, living on the level of some animal. Or a defeated farmer like King Wallace, bent and broken by the backbreaking labor in fields that would never make him more than starving white trash.

It was an old thought pattern for Garland. He rose from his desk, unable to remain still with the restlessness of it. The sun shone obliquely on the building, making a brazen smash of light against the small leaded panes of the windows. He opened a window, squinting against the afternoon brightness to look down the river road toward the Manatte plantation.

He had tried to see Corsica several times since they had met at Mock's ten days ago, but Dee had always met him on the porch and told him Corsica was upstairs. That filled Garland with a bitter anger. She'd come down well enough when this was finished. She'd see how she had misjudged him!

Movement in the street below took up his attention. Harry Sharp was riding in from the west, impeccably tailored as ever in his dove-gray fustian and gleaming Panama hat. He rolled drunkenly in the saddle, hailing everybody on the street. Obermeier came out of Deller's store and dumped a package in his buckboard at the curb.

"Ho, Harry," he shouted. "What are you celebrating?"

Sharp reined up before the Clover Saloon, sliding off his horse.

"Beef just dropped two more cents a pound in Kansas City. Come on over and meet your ruin like a gentleman."

Obermeier shook his head, climbing into the wagon. The rig groaned as he clucked the team away from the curb and then set up a subdued rattling as the animals broke into a trot. But Garland was no longer watching that. There were three horses hitched to the rack before Deller's general store. One of them was Tar Baby.

Blacklaws was well then and had returned. *What was he doing in Deller's store? Getting supplies? Or finding out who had bought the iron latch with so many locks from Deller?*

Charlie Carew ambled out of the two-by-four Association office, pinched in between the Clover and the harness shop. He stood on the curb for a moment, idly surveying the street, pasty jowls bulging as he chewed on a cigar. At last he took this out and bent to spit, lifting one hand to keep his archaic stovepipe hat on the protuberant bulge of his skull.

At this moment Blacklaws came from the shadowed doorway of the store across the street and stepped off the curb to his horse. He was carrying no packages. For just an instant his gaze swept up to the windows of Garland's office.

Carew straightened from spitting to replace his cigar again. He squinted against the sun, watching Blacklaws climb aboard Tar Baby. The man seemed unable to put much weight on his right leg. Once aboard, however, his heavy body settled into the saddle with the casual ease so typical of him. He nodded perfunctorily at the stock detective as he wheeled the black mare around and then lined out down the street toward the river. Carew watched Blacklaws out of sight, chewing on his stogie. Then he drew it from his mouth, looking at it with disgust, and flung it into the street. After this he turned to amble back into the Association office.

Garland watched this absently, his mind on the other man. *So Blacklaws knew he had gotten the latch from Deller's store. What would that mean? Simply that Blacklaws now realized Garland wanted him dead. Perhaps Blacklaws had guessed that before. But now he knew for sure.*

Garland left the window and tried to go back to work. But there was nothing important to do, and that obscure restlessness still stirred him. Finally he got his slouch hat and locked up the office. He had been meaning to go to the Manattes, and today was as good a time as any.

All the way out, obscure thoughts of Blacklaws stirred in Garland's mind. Ever since that night at Mock's, he had known he was going to kill the man. It had first come to him on the impulse of anger. But even later, when he had calmed down and was thinking of it in the quiet of his home or riding into town, he felt little surprise that the idea could present itself without any particular shock. Never an introspective man, he accepted it calmly, without trying to analyze what effects it had or didn't have on him. Perhaps it was such a natural culmination of so many years of hatred and antagonism that all impact was gone from its final appearance.

151

A dozen plans had occurred to him. He had thought of simply going out to Mock's and getting Blacklaws. But he doubted if he could find the way again. And he wanted no witnesses. He had considered staking out the line shack at Smoky Canes. But he had no idea when Blacklaws would come back. *It would have to be something like Tate had set up. Only better. Infinitely better. Because Blacklaws would be on his guard now more than ever. Garland would have to know exactly where Blacklaws would be at a given time, and it would have to be a place in which there was no danger of discovery, at that time or afterward.*

All this was still moving turgidly through him when he turned off the river road into the *allée*, and the roof of the Manatte house, with its crumbling pantiles, came into view above the trees ahead. Garland was still in the drive between the post oaks when he caught sight of Corsica and her father on the porch. She was bending over his cane chair with an intense expression on her face, saying something. Garland could not hear them, but he did not think they had seen him. He pulled off the winding drive into the oaks and dense brush, dismounting and ground-hitching his horse and then moving through the trees on foot. Finally he was near enough to hear Corsica's voice.

"Are you sure, Dad? Why didn't you tell me before? You know how long I've been trying to get it out of you."

"Why should I tell you?" quavered Troy Manatte. "What's the difference? Why not let the dead past lie . . . ?"

"When it might mean a man's life?" Corsica's voice was brittle with impatient anger. "You know the only reason Kenny isn't up for trial now is that they never had any evidence."

"Oh no, Corsica, it ain't that bad. . . ."

"You know it is. Now you've got to remember this, Dad, you've got to remember what you told me."

"Sure I'll remember. Think I'm getting old or something?"

Peering through the bushes, Garland saw Corsica turn and go into the house, leaving the front door open. He heard her heels tap on the entrance hall floor then go up the stairs. Garland went through the remaining trees at a long-legged walk, past the rusty ring posts and up the sagging steps. He peered through the French doors to make sure nobody else was in the parlor. Then he went to Troy Manatte at the far end of the gallery. The old man looked up vaguely.

"Well? Quintin, I thought you was branding this afternoon."

Garland put his hand on Troy's shoulder. "I haven't had anything to brand in ten years."

The old man winced. "Not so hard, Quintin. What's the matter?"

"What were you and Corsica talking about?" Garland asked.

Troy sat staring off at the grove so long Garland thought he would not answer. Then he started faintly. "Corsica?" he asked. "She hasn't been here all afternoon. She and her ma went off to the cotillion at the Roman place."

"Troy,"—Garland's voice was sharp with impatience—"John Roman hasn't given a cotillion since 1866. Come out of it, will you? Corsica was here, talking to you, only a couple of minutes ago."

"I can't recollect."

"Listen, you old fool . . . !"

"Let go, Quintin. You're hurting me."

Garland straightened up from the old man. It seemed he had heard steps in the entrance hall. He turned to see Corsica standing there. She was dressed in a simple flowered print that clung faithfully to the curve of her full hips and the swell of her breasts. Anger gave the oblique planes of her cheeks a glowing tint.

"What are you doing, Quintin?"

"When'd you get back from the cotillion, honey?" Troy asked.

She frowned at her father. "What were you trying to get out of him, Quintin?" Her eyes widened. "You overheard us?"

"Suppose I did."

"I would have seen you that close on the drive," she said. "You were hiding. You must have been. In the trees."

"All right," he said impatiently, "I eavesdropped. It's come to that, Corsica, when you won't trust me any more. You've misjudged me completely. You haven't even given me a chance to defend myself. Your whole idea about what I did with Phil is wrong."

"I don't want to talk about it."

"Please, Corsica. Let me see you alone. I've got to."

She gazed at him in a somber anger that turned her dark eyes almost opaque. Then she shrugged and turned inside. The flowered dress made a sibilant sound across the movement of her ripe hips, leading him into the hall and through the parlor door. Within the parlor she turned to face him, waiting stonily. He reached out to catch her arm.

"Corsica, tell me the truth. After thinking it over, can't you see how Mock and Blacklaws twisted things out there in the shack?"

"No," she said.

"Roman and the sheriff and Obermeier and all of them were after Phil, Corsica. He was sitting there in my house with that bullet in him when they came. One slip and they would have found out. He was close to passing out. They would have strung me up along with him. The feeling's that high against the rustlers.''

"Is it?"

"You're refusing to see it. You're letting what Kenny and Mock said blind you."

"Maybe I've been blind up to now. Maybe they opened my eyes. You were fine and noble when you came back from Austin, weren't you, Quintin? Put up such a gallant battle for all the little operators. Painted such a wonderful future for us after you had smashed Roman and made Copper Bluffs decent for the small people again. Everybody admired you so. Until the big ranchers started putting on the pressure. Then you began to come apart at the seams, Quintin. I guess the first time I really began to doubt you was in your office, when they'd just decided to hang Jesse Tanner. All you could worry about was that you'd lost a case. I guess that business with Phil made me see you for what you are. I can't think of a lower thing you could have done. Killing him would have been better. Just shooting him and getting it over with quickly. It makes me sick every time I think what that ride down to Mock's must have done to him. . . ."

"Corsica, stop it."

"Why?" Her whole body was drawn up. "Does it hurt to see yourself so clearly?"

"Corsica . . . !" Little muscles in his cheek twitched as he forced the smile that had always worked such wonders before. He tried to draw her in, suddenly conscious of the satiny texture of her arm against his hand. "Corsica, you can't mean all this, you know you can't, a woman in love. . . ."

"Love?"

The acrid tone of her voice stopped him. He held her body there, so close the soft peaks of her breasts were touching his chest. She did not fight him, but there was an unrelenting rigidity to her body that held him away

155

more strongly than would have any struggle.

"You said you loved me . . . once," he murmured.

"I was a fool then." She spoke through stiff lips. "I didn't even know what love was."

He let her ease away from him slowly, without releasing her arm. "And now," he said softly, "*you do*?"

Her chin lifted sharply. "What if I do?"

"Blacklaws! I knew it! You've been whoring with Blacklaws!" It escaped him sharply. Something flashed in her eyes, but she did not answer him. She remained there in his grip, arched away from him, her eyes meeting his squarely with a scornful defiance. He let her go then, and she stepped back, still looking at him. "Your carnal passion for that filthy swine has come between us? Is that it, Corsica?" Garland demanded.

An incredulous light replaced the scorn in her eyes. Then she let out a throaty laugh.

"I said your carnal passion for that filthy swine has come between us!" Garland's voice had risen.

"You fool!" She said it almost savagely, turning away from him to walk across the room to the divan and then turning back. "My 'carnal passion,' as you call it, hasn't come between us. You did that all by yourself. You showed me exactly what you were more clearly than Mock or Blacklaws could . . . if they'd talked for a week. Whether I'm in love with Kenny, or what's happened between us is none of your business, and it doesn't matter at all."

"It does! If you hadn't been duped into thinking you loved him, he couldn't have set you against me this way. None of this would have happened without him."

She shook her head, staring at him with wide eyes. "You really believe that, don't you?"

"Believe it? *I know it!* Corsica, how can you feel anything for that murdering, misbegotten swine, how can you . . . ?"

The expression in her eyes finally stopped him. It wasn't anger now or scorn. It was pity. It withdrew her from him more completely than anything else could have done. He started to hold out his hand in some irrelevant effort to bridge the gap. Then he dropped the hand and turned to go out, thinking that Blacklaws had done this. Would it never be anything but Blacklaws? It filled him with a bitter need to smash the man, to get him out of the way somehow, a need more intense than he had ever felt before.

He reached his horse, lifted the reins, and turned to mount. The monotonous creak of Troy Manatte's rocker came from the end of the gallery. Through the French windows, Garland could see Corsica at the desk in one corner of the parlor, writing. As she wrote, she turned her head over one shoulder and called something out to the hall. In another moment Dee came into the parlor. Corsica put the paper in an envelope, sealed it, then turned to hand it to Dee. There was an argument. She said something that brought an angry expression to his face. Then Dee shrugged sullenly and turned to go.

Garland hardly expected the man to come out front, but he waited anyway. The only ones she could be writing to were Phil, down at Mock's, or Blacklaws. And with Blacklaws still in his mind, Garland wanted to see that note. What could be so urgent? Was it connected with what she and her father had been talking about?

When Dee did not come out the front door, Garland circled around the house, walking through the grove to the corrals out back. Dee was saddling up a claybank in one of the pens.

It was hidden from the house by the sheds, and Garland went through one of these outbuildings, filled with the heated stench of decaying sawdust and hay and droppings, to come out in the pen. Dee saw Garland, but he finished tugging his latigo tight.

"Who is that note to?" Garland asked.

"Well,"—Dee let it out on a mocking breath—"spying on us now."

"Give it to me, Dee."

"The hell I will," Dee said, turning to mount.

Garland stepped in to catch his arm, preventing his upward movement. "I said, give it to me, Dee."

With a curse, Dee swung back into him, bringing his free arm around to smash Garland across the side of the head. Garland threw up his right arm to block the blow and came in under it at the same time to sink his left viciously in Dee's stomach.

Dee gasped and came over against him. Garland caught his long hair and pulled his head down till he was doubled over and hit him behind the neck. Then he took a step back and let Dee fall onto his face. Dee lay there, face buried in the sawdust, making retching sounds. Garland bent, rolled him over, and fished in his pockets for the note. He ripped the sealed envelope open. The note was to Blacklaws. Corsica asked him to come to the Manatte house immediately, saying it was something terribly important.

Dee rolled over, spitting sawdust. Pain squinted his eyes shut, and he held one hand against the back of his neck.

"You've broke it," he groaned.

"I don't think so." Garland dropped the note and torn envelope in Dee's lap. "It wasn't what I was looking for."

Dee had trouble getting to his feet. He swayed faintly, making no attempt to pick up the letter and envelope that had fallen from his lap. Bitter anger robbed his face of all its sardonic mockery, and it seemed hard for him to breathe.

"I won't forget this, Quintin," he said. "As long as I live, I won't forget it."

"Do what you like," Garland shrugged. He turned away and went back through the sheds to the grove. With the defeat and bitterness of all the past years and of today seething at him—the murder of his father, the fact that Blacklaws might well find the packery and ruin his last chance here, the final blow of seeing how he was losing Corsica to the man—Garland knew a savage welcome of the chance this note brought. It answered all the qualifications. Blacklaws would be coming to the Manattes' within the limits of a definite time and by a definite route. It was what Garland had been waiting for.

He got his horse and left the Manattes', heading north along the river road to reach his home. And he was thinking. *Blacklaws would be home. The man might have recovered, but he couldn't have been out of bed many days, and the ride into town would have been enough for him. So he'd be there at the line shack when Dee reached it. And Dee? His pride might prevent him from telling exactly what happened in the corral. But he was just malicious enough to let Blacklaws know that Garland had seen the note.*

Now Garland came to the stalk itself, and he was using all his intimate knowledge of Blacklaws and the processes of the man's mind. *It was almost a certainty that, with Tate having failed, Blacklaws would assume for caution's sake that Garland was now ready to do the job himself. So all of Blacklaws's moves would be made with that in mind.*

Garland had been associated with enough lawmen during his legal practice to know the basic precepts in manhunting. Outguessing a man was like taking steps, one after the other. *The first step a hunted man would take was the most natural one—to hide. The hunter would expect him to do this and would be looking for him in places which offered the most concealment. Thus, in trying to outguess his stalker, the hunted man would*

159

go a step further, avoiding the logical hiding places and seek a place so obvious the hunter would not expect him to be there.

The swampy character of the country around the Sabine made it almost mandatory that a man stick to well-known trails if he had a long distance to go. There were two trails to the Manatte place from Smoky Canes. One lay north along the Neches River, to the Houston road, then east along this through Copper Bluffs and down the Sabine road to the Manatte house. It was a circuitous route, the longest way around, and the most secretive. Thus it was that first step in the game—the most logical trail for a hunted man to seek.

The other route was east along the cattle trail to the Sabine and then north along the Sabine road to the Manatte place. This was the shortest, the most open to ambush—and the least likely trail a hunted man would take. Under ordinary circumstances that's exactly why Blacklaws would take it. But these weren't ordinary circumstances. Blacklaws knew he wasn't being hunted by an ordinary man. He was being hunted by a man who knew better than anyone else in the world how his mind worked. So what would Blacklaws do? He'd pull another switch.

He'd think that Garland would expect him to take the cattle trail to the Sabine road. He'd go a step farther and choose the route he would have ordinarily avoided. The Neches-Houston road. Thus Garland reasoned. It was a complex progression of logic, and only a man who knew Blacklaws as well as Garland did would be so sure of its conclusion. But once having reached it, he based all the rest of his plans surely upon the premise that Blacklaws would take the Neches-Houston road.

It took a half hour of hard riding for Garland to reach his own home at the head of Bayou Lafitte. He went inside to get the old Spencer repeater his father had brought back from the war. He got three tubes of cartridges from the Blakeslee box on the shelf and slipped them into a coat pocket. Then he went out to the gear in the breezeway and found the rifle boot mashed beneath the saddles and other gear. He lashed this on under his left stirrup leather, shoved the Spencer home, and got back on his horse.

Again his mind was on Blacklaws. *Suppose by some wild chance the man got through to the Manattes' and then trailed him from there. It was a long shot, but Garland wouldn't overlook it. He would even plant this trail to outguess Blacklaws.*

Garland wanted to get him even if he came by this route. So he'd have to plant sign that would lead Blacklaws into the trap. He hadn't bothered doing anything with the trail he had left from the Manatte house to his own home. That was a logical destination for him. But from here on out he'd make it look as if he were trying to hide his trail, as if he really did not want Blacklaws to come up on him from behind. Yet he'd leave just enough sign, as if he had slipped up here and there, to lead Blacklaws in a definite direction.

So he'd start by heading directly away from his true objective. That was a logical thing for a man trying to hide his trail. It took him ten minutes to reach the Houston road, riding through shale and loblolly and what water he could find in an effort to cover his tracks. He knew there was no reason deliberately to leave sign. As hard as he tried, he would inevitably drop a mark here or there that Blacklaws would pick up.

Reaching the Houston road, he turned east toward Copper Bluffs, instead of west toward the Neches, which was his true goal. He kept carefully to the myriad tracks already in the road. It would take a tracker of uncommon skill to separate his marks from the others. Finally he hit the upper reaches of Mexican Creek. He turned south in the shallows of this. There were narrow sections where he could not get through without brushing the overhanging foliage. Blacklaws would think himself very clever, picking up such obscure traces. Suddenly, splashing along through the shallows and leaving all these signs that would lead a man to his death, Garland found himself smiling.

Chapter Sixteen

Blacklaws had expected Charlie Carew to pick him up along the trail after leaving town, but the man did not show. Blacklaws reached his shack by Smoky Canes, unsaddled, and then got a chair from inside, putting it against the wall by the door. Here he sat with his healing leg thrust out straight in front of him, building a smoke and waiting for Carew.

The heat of the afternoon sun settled his heavy body in the chair with that utter relaxation of which he was so capable. Its light, turned mealy by a fine haze, cast angular shadows deeply across the left side of his face, accenting its blunt strength. He was sitting that way when Dee Manatte broke from the loblollies at a hard gallop and swung his claybank into a hock-scraping halt before Blacklaws, swinging off. The horse stood lathered and trembling behind him while he pulled the note from his pocket.

"Corsica sent it. I don't know what it's about."

Blacklaws took the paper, unfolded and read it.

"She wants me to come to your place right away," he said.

"Yeah." A sly relish curled Dee's lips. "Garland was mighty interested."

Blacklaws looked up. "Garland?"

Dee's grin was sardonic. "Corsica wouldn't tell him what it was all about."

"But Garland did know she asked me to come."

"Yeah." Dee studied his face with narrow eyes a moment, then added: "Corsica wants me to ride for the sheriff too. I don't know why. My horse is about played out."

"So I see."

"Can I use Tar Baby? You haven't got to go as far as I have."

"Not the way you treat horses, Dee."

A momentary anger pinched in Dee's cheeks. Then he snorted disgustedly and turned back to the claybank. With one foot lifted into the stirrup, he turned to look back over his shoulder. "You going?"

"I'll be there."

"Fine," Dee smiled. There was some secret enjoyment in his voice. "I'll see you."

He swung around and went up with a lash of his right leg that took him into the saddle hard. The nervous beast whirled and broke into a frantic gallop with Dee's spurs at her flanks. Blacklaws watched a moment with his own disgust for a man who would handle his animal that way. Then he turned to limp inside after his saddle. It was heavy work, with his bad leg, getting it out and onto the horse. As he did it, his mind was at work.

Garland wants me dead. That's obvious. Deller said he was the only one to buy a latch in the last three months. So he tried to get Tate to kill me, and that failed. Will he try it himself now? I've got to figure on it, any-

*way. From here on out I've got to go on the assumption
that he's out there waiting to kill me.*

*Take today. He knows I'm coming. There are only two
feasible trails. Which one would he choose, if he was
setting up an ambush? He'll be putting himself in my
mind. He'll know that under ordinary circumstances I'd
immediately cross off the Neches-Houston road because
that's the first place another man would pick, and the
first place the man stalking him would look. So that
leaves the cattle trail to the Sabine road. But Garland
figures that I know he's put himself in my mind. He'll
expect me to go one step farther to outguess him. He'll
expect me to pull another switch and go right back to
the Neches-Houston road. If he means to do it today,
that's where he'll be waiting.*

Blacklaws led Tar Baby out of the corral, stepped
aboard, and sat heavily in the saddle, staring off toward
the west. For a moment he had the impulse to call Garland's bluff and take the Neches-Houston route. Then
he shook his head savagely. *You can't make me do that,
Quintin, he thought. You can't make me mad enough to
kill you, and you can't put me in a position where I have
to kill you to save my own skin. So sit out there and
stew, damn you.*

He turned the black mare east along the cattle trail
until he reached the Sabine and then turned north along
this through the last heat of the afternoon. He tried to
take the usual pleasure spring in this land brought him.
The river was swollen and turbulent and young again,
undercutting its banks till big chunks of mud slid off
into the yellow-streaked water like layers sliced from a
chocolate cake. A million young leaves were pushing
the old ones off the live oaks, and jasmine twined its
lemon streamers around the twisted myrtle trunks. The
faint reek of turpentine reached him whenever he passed
a stand of longleaf pine, and it seemed the woodpeckers

were never still. But somehow Garland kept entering his mind to spoil it all.

He broke off the river road before he came within sight of the Manatte place and walked Tar Baby up one of the back trails, hitching the mare in timber on the edge of what had once been the cotton fields. From here he walked around the fringe of the trees to the front of the house.

Through the French windows Blacklaws could see Troy Manatte sitting on the divan and Corsica pacing back and forth in front of the mantel. Blacklaws continued his walk, about a hundred yards away from the house, circling it completely, stopping every few feet to look for sign. No fresh marks and, if a man had been hidden here to shoot, Blacklaws would have come across him. He finally came back to the *allée*. Corsica had stopped pacing now and was talking with her father, bent toward him with intensity.

"Stay easy, Kenny."

Blacklaws felt tension grip him at the voice from behind. Then, as nothing more came, he turned. Sheriff Waco Sheridan stood twenty feet off in the trees, a stooped shape in the shadows with that inevitable pursed expression of his lips, like a man without his uppers.

"You're getting to be the most suspicious man, Kenny," he said. "What were you looking for this time?"

Blacklaws shrugged. "You're an Indian, Waco."

"Choctaw," said Waco, unsmiling. He came forward, peering at Blacklaws's face. "Couldn't quite figger out what kind of roundup this was. Thought I'd have a look-see myself before I stepped in the pen. Everything in order?"

"I couldn't beat any snakes out of the brush."

Waco tilted his head to one side, calling back over his shoulder. "Come on in, Cam."

Cameron and Dee Manatte appeared. The deputy was leading Sheridan's horse. Dee's claybank was yellow with dirty lather and still trembling. He hauled it up sharply when he saw Blacklaws.

"You really got here," he said.

Blacklaws tilted his head up, eyes heavily lidded. "Didn't you expect me to?" he asked.

Dee studied him a moment in a puzzled way. "I never know what to expect from you, Kenny," he said with a faint wonder riding his voice.

Blacklaws got Tar Baby and hitched her to the rusty ring posts with the other animals, and then the four men went in. Corsica met them at the living-room door, expectancy lying pale and tense in her face. The ripeness of her body in its clinging flowered print drove everything else from Blacklaws's mind for a moment.

"Well, boys," Troy said, looking up brightly as they entered the living room, "come for that poker game?"

Corsica turned to her father with a sharp sound of impatience. "Dad, I want you to tell the sheriff exactly what you told me on the porch this afternoon."

"I was riding this afternoon, don't you remember? Aren't you going to offer the boys drinks before we break out the cards?"

"Dad." The angry impatience pinched at her voice. "This afternoon, on the porch, you told me. . . ." She broke off, whirling at Sheridan. "I want him to tell you of his own accord. I don't want you to think I've put any of it in his head. It's what I've been trying to get out of him for years, Waco. He's an old man, and he's tired, and his mind plays him tricks. But it isn't only that. He's afraid. He's got sort of an obsession. Whenever he does remember it, he's got that obsession, he's just so afraid. . . ."

Sheridan frowned at her then went over to sit down

beside the old man. "Now look, Troy, what's this all about?"

Troy shook his head vaguely. "If you didn't come for that poker game, why did you come?"

"Tell me a couple of things, Corsica," Sheridan said.

"Martin Garland. Tate." The last left her in a strained whisper. "Bayou Lafitte."

Blacklaws could not help looking at her sharply. She met his gaze with her eyes filled by some luminous plea. Dee slouched over to the wing chair and dropped into it. "I'll be damned," he said.

"What about Martin Garland and Tate?" Sheridan asked Troy.

The old man's senile face twisted into a frown, and he began to shake his head from side to side. Sheridan's eyes swung up to Blacklaws. "It might mean a man's whole life, Troy," he said softly. "You haven't the right to conceal a thing like that."

A childish grimace compressed Troy's face. It reminded Blacklaws of a kid just before he broke into tears.

"I'm an old man," he whispered. "My mind ain't as good as it used to be. I can't remember what I said."

"You mean you're afraid to remember?"

"All right. So I'm afraid. Somebody will hurt me. I can't remember anything else, but I know somebody will come after me and kill me if I tell who killed Martin Garland . . . !"

His head raised sharply, eyes widening. He stared around at them. Then he lunged out of the divan suddenly. He almost pitched on his face before he grabbed one of the lyre arms and found his balance. Then he walked toward the mantel, stooped deeply, and caught at its edge. He stood against the mantel, faced away from them, trembling in a palsied way.

"Troy," said Sheridan, "I'll give you my promise of

personal protection, if that's what it will take. If you know who killed Garland, we won't rest till we get him.''

''Nobody can get him.'' Troy's voice came out in a shrill wheeze. ''He's a devil. He's accounted for more than one of those men that's disappeared out in the bogs. He's got that thing in his mind about whoever tampers with his hogs. You know how he is about that.''

''You're talking about Tate, now?''

''I knew Martin had killed one of his hogs.'' Troy was babbling now, the words spilling out over one another so fast they were hardly intelligible. ''I guess nobody else ever knew. But I was with Martin on that hog hunt when he killed one of Tate's hogs. I was always scared Tate would get even. Then, a couple of months later, Martin wanted a loan. I rode over with it. Came up to the house . . . heard somebody shout down in the bayou . . . went down there afoot. Martin was whaling Kenny with that bullwhip . . . they didn't see me. Kenny took the whip right in his face so's he could jump Martin. Martin went over backward and hit his head. He didn't move after that. There was a lot of blood. I never saw a kid so scared. Kenny must have thought he had killed Martin. He turned and ran. . . .'' Troy broke off sobbing, his hands gripping the mantel tightly.

''What about Tate?'' asked Sheridan.

''After Kenny disappeared, I saw Martin roll over. I guess I was more afraid of what would happen to Kenny than Martin. He was running off so crazy anything could have got him out in those bogs. A 'gator, quicksand, the moccasins. I ran after to tell him he hadn't killed Martin. I was old then too. I got winded pretty quick and fell down. When I got my strength back, I had to turn around and went back to Martin. I saw the whole thing through the trees. I . . . I. . . .''

Corsica was bent forward, face taut with her plea. "Dad."

Troy shook his head as if in pain. "Tate was bent over Martin. He had a big rock in his hand. He must have seen the whip and figured out what had happened between Kenny and Martin. He knew Kenny'd be blamed if Martin was found dead down there with that whip. So he beat Martin's head in. When he heard me coming, he dropped the rock. I had a gun, or I guess he would've jumped me too. I couldn't get him, though. He got away."

Sheridan leaned toward him. "Why didn't you tell, Troy? Why in God's name didn't you tell?"

"He got Martin, didn't he?" panted Troy. "He'd get me too if I told. I was an old man even then, Sheridan. You don't know how it tore me. I took the whip to keep the stain off Kenny as much as I could. I was at the point of telling a half a dozen times after, Sheridan. You've got to believe me. But Kenny had disappeared, and I couldn't see what good it'd do, other than put Tate on my trail. Tate got Martin, didn't he? Got all those other men. He'd do the same thing to me if I told. No lawman could get him. I'd be afraid to go out this door. I'd be afraid, Sheridan. . . ."

Troy trailed off, pinching at the mantel with those frail hands. Corsica went to him, taking his arm to turn him around so she could hold him. He pulled away, and Blacklaws could see the soundless tears squeezed out of his squinting eyes. He stared pathetically at Sheridan.

"You won't make me tell, will you, Sheriff? Please don't make me tell . . . !"

Corsica's voice was low and shaken. "I'll take him upstairs."

She led him through them to the doorway and out of sight. Deep thought gave Sheridan's face that pouting expression. Then he raised his speculative eyes to Blacklaws.

"How do you feel, Kenny?"

Blacklaws frowned, trying to identify what he felt. Somewhere within him was a deep mingling of emotions. He could not separate them yet or identify them. He could not find the immense relief he knew he should feel. Perhaps the surprise was too great to leave room for feelings yet.

He had a need to be alone. He stared around at the three men, opened his mouth to say something then, without saying it, he turned and went out. He was almost to the ring posts when he heard the sound of Corsica's footsteps on the gallery behind him. He halted, turning slowly to meet her. She came up to him till the swell of her breasts touched him. The blood thickened in his throat. Her face, upturned to him in the dusky afternoon, had the texture of velvet.

"I wish I could say what's inside me, Kenny. There aren't any words. I want to laugh. I want to cry." She took a deep breath, shaking her head. "I wish I could have done this nine years ago . . . for you."

"You've done it now, that's all that matters. I owe you more thanks than I can ever give." He took her by the arms, and their satiny warmth seemed to flow through his whole body. "I've got to tell you this, Corsica. It makes me feel terrible, but I've got to tell you. I thought you deliberately sent me out to Chenière Dominique."

"I can't blame you, Kenny," she said. "It was just a part of the whole thing that happened to you. I was right, wasn't I? You weren't only afraid of the anger Quintin could draw from you. You were afraid of all other emotions, too."

"I suppose so," he said. "It got so mixed up in me, Corsica."

"Of course it did. You were suffering from a terrible sense of guilt. Some men might have gone to pieces under it. You fought it, and that's what it did to you. But now you know you're not guilty, Kenny. You don't have to fight it any more. We can face each other clearly. Nothing's between us."

He found himself pulling away. Nothing? He suddenly realized why he had not felt the relief he should have felt at finding he was not the killer of Martin Garland. There was still something unresolved. Now that the sense of guilt was gone, what would he feel toward Quintin Garland? Had the anger Quintin could draw from him known its source in that sense of guilt? Or was it more than that? Had his avoidance of Quintin today been the result of a calm, logical process of mind, or were its roots in fear? Again he had come to that point beyond which his mind would offer no answers. He could conjecture all night and never really find out what was going on inside him. There was only one way to settle the whole thing.

"Corsica," he said, stepping back, "there's something I've got to do."

He saw the disappointment start in her face. Then her eyes, searching his, widened with understanding.

"Quintin?" she said softly.

"It's got to be answered."

Fear shone in her eyes, and she reached out for him. "Kenny. . . ."

"I've got to do it, Corsica."

He turned away, wishing he could explain it to her, but it was something a man could not tell anyone else. They would have had to live with it for nine years, as he had, borne down by it, haunted by it day and night, kept by it from the land he loved. He unhitched his mare and swung aboard. He looked down at her upturned face for a last moment. That she had ceased trying to stop

171

him gave Blacklaws a truer measure of Corsica's understanding than he had known before.

He turned Tar Baby and headed her at a canter down the *allée* to the river road. He came around the last post oak into sight of the Sabine, and Tar Baby almost pitched him off her rump, rearing up. He fought the animal around and finally got it down on all four feet again, fretting and dancing. It was Charlie Carew who had startled the animal. He sat at the edge of the road, heavy-bellied body slack in the saddle of his horse, chewing complacently on his unlit cigar.

"Saw Dee come to town hell-for-leather after the sheriff," he said. "Thought I'd see what was up."

Blacklaws's weight settled into his rigging with a muffled creaking, his face somber. "Troy Manatte just told Sheridan that he saw Tate kill Martin Garland." Something fluttered through Carew's squinted eyes. Finally he reached up to remove his cigar, spitting aside. Then he took a heavy breath. "Detecting's a dirty business," he said.

Blacklaws continued to stare flatly at the man, his lips shaping the words without much movement. "Did you know the whole story?"

Carew replaced his cigar, studying Blacklaws's face. "I pieced most of it together. I was out to the Manattes' with Sheridan one night, and Troy started asking Corsica where his whip was. She cut him off so sharp it put me to figuring. I remembered there had been some talk about Martin Garland's whip missing after his death. Next time I went out to the Manattes', I got Troy alone and put the pressure on. He was scared to death. Enough came out for me to guess the rest."

"And you brought me back here under the threat of exposing me, knowing all the time it was Tate who had killed Garland!"

Carew met his eyes. "You going to bust my guts, Kenny?"

Blacklaws stared at Carew. He could feel no anger at the man. He was just sick of the whole thing and glad to have it finished.

"I ought to," he said.

Carew's kettle belly quivered with his short chuckle. "But you won't. I don't think that was the real reason you come back, anyway. You wasn't as afraid of your own hide as you was of the fact that Corsica might get hurt in this. I wish I'd known how much that meant to you in the first place. I wouldn't have bothered with the other at all." He dipped his head, staring quizzically up at Blacklaws from beneath those hairless brows. "Two hundred and fifty a month, Kenny?"

"You don't have to up to the ante, Charlie." Blacklaws was staring beyond the man. "I'll see it through without that."

Carew's eyes narrowed. "Then you think Corsica's mixed up in it?"

"Not Corsica herself. Phil is. I want to know why. Did you check the Manatte investments?"

"We did. They haven't been paying enough interest during the last few months to feed a heel fly."

Blacklaws nodded. "That's what I thought. And Phil has been giving Corsica the money he makes rustling and convincing her it's interest off the stocks."

Carew shook his head. "Corsica's done a wonderful job of holding that family together with such a small amount coming in. I don't know where they'd turn without it. I think it'd break her heart."

Blacklaws's eyes narrowed. "It would break her heart worse to find out Phil is mixed up in this."

"Maybe he's not mixed up too deep," said Carew. "If the stocks quit paying off only a few months ago, he couldn't have been rustling long."

"Promise me you'll do what you can for him?" said Blacklaws.

"If he'd turn state's evidence, we might even get him off completely," Carew said.

"Who was in the posse that time they found Phil playing cards with Quintin?"

Carew frowned. "Obermeier, and a couple of his riders, Roman and some of his, the sheriff and his deputy."

"Sallier?"

Carew chewed harder on his cigar. "The Creole wasn't along, from what I heard."

"Harry Sharp?"

"Sharp was in town drunk."

"And who was in the posse the time before?"

"The same bunch," said Carew.

"Sallier?"

"I'm not sure."

"Sharp?"

Carew grinned disgustedly. "It would have interrupted his drinking."

Blacklaws nodded. "Next time Roman hits town, raising a posse, I want to know as soon as possible just who is in the posse . . . and who isn't."

Absently, Carew removed his cigar. "What's going through that mind now?"

"It isn't clear yet," Blacklaws told him. "Give me a little time."

Carew turned to stare at his cigar. With a snorting sound, he started to fling the pulpy stub from him. Then he checked himself. "Sure, Kenny," he said, still frowning at the butt. "You got your time." He slowly returned the cigar to his mouth. Then a broad grin spread his jowls. "Just keep figuring at it." He leaned expansively back in the saddle and started chewing on the stogie once more. "That's all I ask, Kenny. Just keep figuring at it."

Chapter Seventeen

The sun was down, but its heat and the last of its reflected light remained. This left a humid mantle of dusk that seemed to stifle all sound and movement on the hogback of land which ran north and south between the Neches River and Bayou Choupique. The two bodies of water ran parallel for half a mile here, so close together that nothing but a narrow shell ridge lay between them. This ridge was hardly wider than the wheel-scarred wagon road that ran its length. On the slopes siding this road enough topsoil had gathered to support some growth, a snarled mat of stunted post oaks and pecans and their underbrush of bindweed and rozo grass.

Once a man gained the road, it was almost impossible to leave it. He could turn neither right nor left without immediately meeting a cliff so steep no horse could keep its balance, and even a man afoot would have great trouble to keep from losing his grip and pitching down. Thus the timber offered no cover, for it grew on this slope, and a man could not gain it without falling off the road. A knob of pecans and palmettos at the northern extremity of the ridge commanded the road for a great distance. This was where Garland had hidden himself.

It had been the guessing game again. The place was ideal for ambush. He was completely concealed. A man coming from the south had no cover, could not gain any when the firing began without putting himself completely at Garland's mercy. It was the first place an ambusher would pick. It was the first place from which any man experienced in the stalk would expect to be ambushed. That was exactly why Garland had chosen it. Blacklaws would never believe him fool enough to pick such an obvious place.

Time bore down on him now. *How long had he been here? Surely Blacklaws should have come by now. It was almost evening.* Dusk was narrowing his circle of vision. His sweat had dampened the butt of his rifle till the reek of oil and walnut was strong and acrid. The rozo grass was slippery and abrasive against his sodden clothes. It filled him with a maddening impulse to move.

He knew how foolish that would be. It could not last much longer. He had to keep perfectly still. He had set it up so carefully now, and Blacklaws would walk right into it.

After leaving Carew, Blacklaws pushed his mare on up the river road toward Copper Bluffs. If Garland had gone home after leaving the Manatte house earlier in the afternoon, he would have taken this route. Blacklaws substantiated that by dismounting to sift out Garland's sign from the other tracks in the road. In the failing light it was hard to see, but he finally found the mark of a feather-edged horseshoe. Garland had left this sign at Mock's, and Blacklaws had picked it up in enough other places to know it meant the Copperbottom.

He reached Garland's house with dusk creeping over the land. He hitched Tar Baby in the timber and then took the necessary precautions to make sure nobody was home. The gaunted mare was the only horse in the corral, but Blacklaws still took no chances. He came up on the blind side of the shack after making sure the timber was empty around the house. He took still longer to make sure nobody was inside. Finally he stepped in and lit a match. It required but a moment of light to see what he wanted. Martin Garland's old Spencer repeater was gone from its horn rack on the wall.

Blacklaws shook out the match and stepped outside. It was going through his head now. *So Garland's waiting for me somewhere along the Neches-Houston route. He's been clever up to now. He won't overlook the slim possibility that I might get through somehow and come up on him from this direction. So what'll he do with his trail away from here?*

Garland's tracks heading away from the house were clear. Blacklaws got Tar Baby and followed them out onto the trail that led back to the Houston road. It took him into a grove of loblollies. He lost it and had to dismount and circle to pick it up again. At last he realized that Garland was trying to hide his trail. That was natural. But it was not quite right.

Blacklaws reached the Houston road and finally made out the tracks heading east toward Copper Bluffs. Again that was natural. If a man's true objective was the Neches, an obvious step in throwing off pursuit would be to turn in exactly the opposite direction. Instead of trying to follow the prints in the myriad other signs on the road, Blacklaws kept his eye peeled for where Garland might have turned off. Reaching Mexican Creek, he found that Garland went in but did not come out. The man had turned upstream or down to hide his tracks in water. Downstream would take him in the direction of the Neches. Blacklaws turned this way. A hundred yards of riding the shallows and he found where overhanging *agrito* had scraped against something at the height of a horse's flank.

Now it was going through his mind again. *What's Quintin doing? On the surface he's a man trying like hell to hide his trail. But he must know he can't hide it completely. He hasn't time, if he wants to reach the*

Neches ahead of me. So he doesn't really want to hide his sign. He just wants to make me think he's trying to. Why?

A tracker went on one of two premises in such a case as this. Either the man he was following had tried to hide the sign or was using it to lure the tracker into a trap. If a man was trying to hide his sign, he obviously did not want the tracker to follow him and therefore could not use the trail as a decoy.

That's what Garland wants to put in my mind, thought Blacklaws. *He figures that if I think he's really trying to hide the trail, I won't be looking for it to lead me into a trap.*

Chapter Eighteen

The night had come now. The velvety texture of its blackness pushed insistently against Garland, where he lay in the rozo grass, as if to mock him for his incapacity to see. The chirping of crickets formed a shrill cacophony that never seemed to cease. The moon should be up in a few minutes. He would know what time it was then. He shifted impatiently and quit trying to see anything along the road. It was too late anyway. Whether the moon rose or not, it was too late. Blacklaws would have come by now. There was only one chance left.

Garland turned his head to look down over the land through which his back trail came. Perhaps Blacklaws would still come that way. If Blacklaws knew Garland was out here and had somehow taken the Sabine road and gotten through to the Manatte house, there was still a chance that he would track Garland home and then out here. Garland found his eyes following the back trail from where it left the trees on the opposite bank of the bayou. He had crossed the water at a ford and had ridden on up to a saddle in the ridge. Garland now was just above the saddle, in his thicket of palmettos and pecans. He had ridden on north and picketed his horse out of sight and earshot and had then returned, but the horse's tracks led through the saddle almost directly past his ambush.

Blacklaws would not expect Garland to choose such an obviously ideal spot for ambush. Garland had figured that out. An ordinary man might have chosen such a spot, but Blacklaws would figure that Garland was too smart for that. He'd think Garland would know it was the first place an experienced stalker would look for an ambush. And, finally, Blacklaws would never believe Garland fool enough to advertise his hiding place by letting the tracks of his horse lead directly into it, even though he was making every attempt to hide those tracks.

So Blacklaws would look for Garland to be somewhere else along the ridge, in a spot so unsuitable for ambush no one would expect it to be there. No timber grew north of the saddle, and soon the ridge itself dropped off into a salt-grass prairie devoid of cover. So it would not be north Blacklaws would be looking but somewhere south of the saddle. And the approach to any of the likely spots down there would lead the man into Garland's vision.

There it was. He had the man coming or going. It gave him a deep satisfaction to go back over every little detail, seeing how cleverly he had worked it out, realizing how inevitable was Blacklaws's death. With a return of his confidence, he realized that perhaps he had been too hasty. Perhaps Blacklaws hadn't been at the line shack after all when Dee came. Maybe Dee had left the note, and Blacklaws had come home later. Maybe he'd still be arriving by the road.

Garland became aware of the great lemon drops splashing the darkness all about him, and he looked up to see that it was the foliage, dappling the light of a rising moon. He stared back down the road, able to see now, and settled himself carefully. *No more moving. It wouldn't be long now. It couldn't be. Just a few minutes. Maybe not even that long.*

He's left the creek here. That's copper hair on the grapevine. It's his Copperbottom all right. Be easier to follow him in the moonlight.

Blacklaws left Mexican Creek on Garland's trail, heading due west now, directly toward the Neches. The moon made a tangled silhouette of the timber and turned the glades and open patches into brazen pools. He could move faster with its illumination, but he didn't get careless. Even though he was sure Garland would be waiting on the Neches road, and this was only a secondary trail, he still kept his cover and did his circling at the open spots and kept throwing out decoys before showing himself.

He did not stick so close to the sign itself now. The direction was fairly obvious, and much of the country was so boggy Garland could have taken only one course through it. Then the bogs fell behind and the timbered prairies began spreading out before Blacklaws.

Finally, threading his way through a dense stand of loblolly and dogwood, he came upon a curving arm of water, its stagnant surface shimmering like black silk in the moonlight. The only water this side of the Neches was Bayou Choupique. He followed its course west through heavy timber. Then, ahead of him, it ran up against a high shell ridge, making a right-angle turn to change its direction and head almost due north along the base of the ridge. Blacklaws knew where he was now. The Neches was on the other side of that ridge, and the wagon road ran along its top.

He got off Tar Baby and made his way afoot through the cover of timber till he came to the turn in the bayou. He knew Garland might well be up on that ridge, and he moved carefully as an Indian, keeping to the shadows and never revealing himself to the high ground. He made his way northward along the bayou till he spotted a ford and then crawled on his belly through the creeper and bindweed till he could look out on this. He soon found the sign Garland had left. The bayou was so narrow at this spot that Blacklaws could see where Garland had gone out of the water on the other side. The man had dismounted and had come back to erase the horse's prints. He had gotten rid of the animal's sign but had been unable to return the mud to its original character. Farther on, the tip of a dogwood branch had been snapped. These signs led Blacklaws's eyes up the shell ridge directly to a saddle. Overlooking the saddle and commanding the road to the south was a mat of palmettos and bindweed which could easily conceal a man.

It's an ideal spot for ambush, Blacklaws thought. *The kind of place an ordinary man would pick. But an experienced hunter would know it was the first place the man he was ambushing would look. Garland would know that.*

Is that what he wants me to think? That he's too smart to pick a place like this. It's what I would ordinarily think. He's tried to make it even more convincing by riding his horse up through the saddle. Only a fool would let his trail lead directly to his ambush. Not a

*man of Garland's intelligence. So you've played the fool,
Quintin, and this is the spot you've picked.*

A cat had begun screaming somewhere out along the
bayou. Its piercing sound kinked at Garland's nerves till
he had the sense of something drawn unbearably taut
within him. His eyes ached with trying to penetrate the
shadows the timber cast farther down the road. *When
would Blacklaws come out of those shadows? It couldn't
be much longer. Or wasn't he coming by the road, after
all?*

For the hundredth time Garland found himself twisting around to stare behind him at his back trail. If Blacklaws was coming from behind, he would come through
timber, to the ford in the bayou, following Garland's
sign, and see the trail crossing the ford and coming right
up through the saddle. Garland had already settled that
in his own mind. *Where would Blacklaws look then?*

North of the saddle the ridge was completely barren,
and the prairie beyond was devoid of cover. So Garland
could not be there. South of the saddle the ridge fell
away in those steep shell cliffs, with timber filling the
hollows and fissures in matted clusters. It would be an
awkward, illogical place for an ambush. For that very
reason, Blacklaws would figure Garland was down there
somewhere. *And how would Blacklaws approach it?*

Garland had that figured out too. *Blacklaws could not
approach the ridge from the north. A snake couldn't get
across that open prairie without being seen. That left
him but one of two routes.*

*To take the first route a man would have to backtrack
through timber till he was out of sight of the ridge then
cross the bayou beyond its turn, where it ran east and
west. Then he would follow the bayou's south bank till
he reached the turn once more. Now he would be on the
inside bank, the one nearest the ridge, in timber that*

grew thickly enough to afford cover all along the base of the ridge. An ordinary man would immediately choose this. It was the safest and provided the most cover, but an experienced stalker would know his ambusher was probably watching that route the closest. So he would take the more exposed and dangerous way, crossing the bayou somewhere near the ford, where he would be least expected to appear.

However; as before, Garland had to go one step farther to account for Blacklaws. *The man would realize Garland had figured it that way, and would pull his usual switch. Instead of taking the route of the experienced hunter, he'd do what he thought Garland would not expect him to do and take the course of the amateur. He would backtrack and cross the bayou where he could not be seen and then come up through the trees on the inside bank.* Thus Garland reasoned.

He settled into the rozo grass again, trying to ease the tension in him. That would not do. He had to be steady when it came. He had it all figured out. He knew the way Blacklaws's mind worked better than anybody else in the world, and he had it all figured out, and he had to be steady when it came. This brought a strange impulse to him. Garland tried to ignore it. He would not be foolish now. But finally he couldn't help answering it. He lifted one hand from the rifle and held it out. It was trembling.

If I remember the spot right, Blacklaws thought, *there's a prairie at the northern tip of that ridge. I couldn't get across there if I was a flea. What does that leave? I could backtrack and cross the bayou out of sight and then come back along the south bank. It would take me right up against the ridge where the bayou turned. But that's the first route a bushwhacker would expect a man to take.*

The bayou here would be the smarter approach. It's almost too exposed to get across. About the only way would be to slip out from that drift log just north of the ford and swim under water to those hyacinths in the middle. Get a breath in them and make it under water to that clump of bindweed on the opposite bank. It's the route a man who knew his stalking would use. Then that's exactly why Garland won't expect me to use it. He looked for me to pull a switch when he figured I'd go by the Neches-Houston route instead of the Sabine road. Now he's figuring I'll pull that same switch here. He'll expect me to do what any amateur would do and come up through those trees on the south bank.

So I'll go back and take Tar Baby across to the south bank. She's just thirsty enough to browse toward water if I turn her loose below the turn in the bayou. Fifty-fifty Quintin will see the movement. Maybe it'll hold his attention enough so I can get across the bayou here.

The cat had stopped screaming. Garland suddenly realized there was no other sound. The crickets had stopped too. *Blacklaws was here.*

A motion in the trees at the base of the ridge caught Garland's eye. He started to turn sharply. He checked himself and moved his head carefully, just enough to see. It was all black mats of shadow and startling patches of moonlight down there, treacherous to the eye.

Then he saw the furtive motion again, coming toward him through those trees along the inside bank of the bayou. Garland felt a vindictive triumph. *Blacklaws had done exactly as he had figured. The man was moving through that timber, looking for Garland somewhere south of the saddle. If he kept coming in this direction, it would lead him right underneath Garland. There would not be twenty feet between them. A perfect shot.*

* * *

184

*You did all right by me, Tar Baby. Garland's watching
those trees. He would have shot if he'd seen me crossing
the bayou. There's enough cover going up the slope to
that saddle now to get right on top of him. But that last
flash of Tar Baby was too near water. I'll have to make
noise if I want to reach Garland before she shows. Then
it all depends on what kind of noise I make.*

Garland licked dry lips, settling himself carefully. That
last motion had been very near thinning timber. *In another moment Blacklaws would unwittingly move into
Garland's sight. He would be screened from farther
down the ridge, where he thought Garland was, but he
would expose himself to the saddle.*

Then a small crackling sound from behind whirled
Garland about. He knew the mistake of such a sharp
movement the instant after he made it. The noise came
again. He started to swing his Spencer around. Then he
checked it. *Blacklaws was too good in the brush to make
that much noise. It didn't have the character of a body
passing through undergrowth. It was a smaller sound.
Like a rattling sound. Like a rock falling through foliage. Could that be it? Could Blacklaws be throwing
rocks over Garland's head to make it sound as if he
were coming in from behind, when really he was still in
those trees below?* Garland turned back the way he had
been watching.

*Quintin's had time to figure it out now. He knows I'm
good enough in the brush so I wouldn't make that much
noise. He'll think those rocks I'm throwing are coming
over his head from the trees below.*

There was another crackling from behind Garland. His
whole body stiffened at repressing an impulse to turn.
Maybe Blacklaws had outguessed him and figured where

*the ambush was, but he knew what the man was doing
now. Blacklaws wanted him to expect it from behind
and, when he was turned that way, would come in on
him from the other direction. Well, he wouldn't panic.
He'd still outguess the man. The last guess was the one
that counted, and he'd kill Blacklaws on it.*

*Give me another second, Tar Baby. He's got his gun on
those trees for good now, and he won't turn around
when I make the noise coming in from behind.*

There was an abrupt motion at the thinning edge of timber. Garland tightened his finger on the trigger. A rider-
less black horse stepped from the trees. Garland felt his
whole body lift in surprise. Then the noise behind blos-
somed into a crash of undergrowth, and he could not
help turning.

"Kenny!"

Blacklaws caught the barrel of the rifle before it could
be swung into him and tore it from Garland's grasp and
threw it aside as he crashed on into the man. Garland
was already coming up out of his crouch into Blacklaws
with that shout still holding his mouth wide open. Blacklaws went into Garland with the man's arms going
around his waist, his momentum carrying the lawyer
backward. They flopped over once with a crashing of
brush and then pitched off the edge of the steep slope.
Grappling, they tumbled down through crushed shells
and bindweed. A mat of palmettos and *agrito* clinging
to the cliff finally caught them for an instant. Blacklaws
tried to tear free of Garland, punching at the man's face.
He felt his blow snap against bone, saw Garland's head
jerk back, but Garland clawed at him, beating at the side
of his head.

It knocked Blacklaws back down and tore both men
free of the tree, and they started rolling again. They car-

omed off another tree. It knocked Garland free, but the slope dropped more steeply, and Blacklaws could not keep himself from rolling on down to the bottom. He flopped through underbrush and crunching shell to end up in the mucky shallows of the bayou.

He rolled to his hands and knees, choking and sputtering. Through blinking eyes he saw Garland coming to his feet out of the water and lunging his way. Blacklaws whirled and tried to rise and meet it, but Garland struck him before he had his feet beneath him. Their combined weight went against Blacklaws's bad leg, and he collapsed. He went under water again with Garland on top. Blacklaws caught one of the man's flailing arms, trying to twist Garland off. His head came out of water. He wanted air so badly he made a broken sobbing sound. Then a smothering weight smashed into his face, putting his head under again.

It was Garland's body, sprawled over his chest and head. Panic gripped Blacklaws. He felt himself start a wild thrashing over which he had no control. Garland fought to keep himself on Blacklaws's head, holding it under with all the weight of his body, beating at Blacklaws. The blood was pounding in Blacklaws's head till he thought it would burst. At last he had to breathe. Water flooded in. Sensation spun. His body writhed in a paroxysm.

With a last desperate upheaval, he shifted enough to get one knee beneath him and to twist a shoulder under Garland. The man tried to drive him down once more, but Blacklaws lunged up beneath him. He tore an arm free and struck at Garland's middle. The lawyer gave a gasp and went backward.

Blacklaws could not rise for a moment. All he could do was crouch there on one knee, coughing and choking, making retching sounds with his effort at sucking in air. He saw Garland coming onto his hands and knees again, spitting mud. He saw Garland getting up to lunge and knew he could never meet it on his bad leg. So he drove to his feet and dove at the man.

He hit Garland amidships, knocking him backward. The man almost went over but caught himself. He struck viciously at the back of Blacklaws's neck. Face buried against Garland's coat, Blacklaws heard his muffled grunt of pain. It stunned him. It cost him agony to gather enough concentration to start driving with his legs. Garland gave him another rabbit punch. It would have knocked Blacklaws down if he hadn't grappled into a clinch with Garland. Now he didn't even know what his body was doing. It was only that one grim idea in his mind—to keep driving, keep driving.

From a vast distance he heard the sloppy sound of his feet in the mud. Then he felt another blow against his neck. But it lacked force. He knew Garland was off balance. The man was tearing at him now instead of hitting, trying to get free and keep his balance at the same time. Arms about the man's waist, Blacklaws churned the water with his driving legs. And finally Garland went over backward. Blacklaws lost his grip and sprawled out on top of the man.

Garland tried to roll over beneath him. Blacklaws smashed at his face. Garland brought a knee up between Blacklaws's legs. The pain of it dropped Blacklaws down on Garland, sickened and helpless. He heard his own groans. He felt Garland's wild struggle to squirm from beneath his dead weight. Finally he felt Garland's hair against his hand. He tangled it through his fingers. He struck feebly at Garland's face with his other hand. From somewhere far off there was an ominous rumbling sound.

Garland's struggles grew wilder. Instead of trying to come up, he was squirming backward, like an eel, trying to get out ahead of Blacklaws. Blacklaws kept his grip on that hair. He had the strength to pull Garland's head up now, so he could strike at it.

"Please, Blacklaws . . . the 'gators!"

"Should have . . . thought of that . . . before!" Blacklaws panted.

With a crazy sound, Garland began fighting him again. Blacklaws was on his hands and knees over the man. Garland tried to pull backward. There was something behind the lawyer. Blacklaws saw that they were up against the huge knees of a cypress. His blow knocked Garland's head back against the gnarled trunk. His fist came away covered with blood.

Unable to go any farther backward, Garland heaved out against him. Blacklaws knocked him back again. Garland was sitting against the tree now, the water up to his chest. He blocked Blacklaws's next blow, tried to catch the arm. Blacklaws let go of Garland's hair and hit him with that fist. He was on his knees astraddle the man now. He kept smashing Garland's head against the tree that way. It was all he could think to do. He was so far gone himself it took the last of his concentration to keep hitting like that. Finally he realized Garland was struggling no longer. He dropped to his hands there in the shallow water, above the man. It was agony trying to get enough air. His whole body swelled and fought for it.

He did not know how long he crouched like that. He heard more alligators lashing the water out in the bayou, and rumbling, and could do nothing about it. After he got his breath, he was still too drained to move. He simply remained there, hoping the alligators would not come.

Finally he gained enough strength to fumble at Garland's hair in the water beneath him. It seemed to take him ages to drag the man out of the water up into the rozo grass. He left Garland on a slant, one arm under

189

his face, so the water would leak out of his mouth. He didn't know whether the man was drowned or not.

He sat down against the bell-shaped trunk of a cypress, dizzy now. Things were far away for a while. The alligators rumbled and thrashed around without coming nearer. Finally Blacklaws saw breath stir Garland's ribs. After a long time Garland belched. He tried to lift himself up. He got twisted around on his side but could not rise. His filmed eyes found Blacklaws. Blacklaws heard his own freakish laughter. It sounded like the gasping of a windsucker.

Garland belched up more water, was sick in the grass. Still Blacklaws could not stop those crazy sounds. It was hysteria now. He was so weak and beaten it was hysteria. Garland finally found his voice.

"What in hell are you laughing at?"

"I'm not mad, Quintin. That's what I'm laughing at. You can't make me mad. All through that fight I wasn't mad. You *can't* make me kill you, and you can't ever make me mad again."

Chapter Nineteen

It was after midnight when Blacklaws got back to the line shack. He was so beaten and exhausted that he could not even unsaddle his horse. He ran Tar Baby into the corral with the kack on and then went inside and threw himself fully clothed onto the bunk. He lay in a half stupor for a while and finally fell asleep. He awoke near noon, stiff and aching in every joint, his body covered with mottled bruises where Garland had pummeled him.

He was surprised, though, at how much the sleep had done for him. It was not the same as that fight with the hogs. He had not actually lost much blood this time, and what wounds his body had were on the surface. The main thing had been the exhaustion, and the slack of that had been taken up overnight.

Now an urgent desire to see Corsica seized him. He could hardly take time to eat breakfast. He was filled with an exalted sense of freedom, as if the fetters of nine years had just been cut loose. He wanted to share it with Corsica, to tell her that what she had said yesterday was fully true now—nothing stood between them.

He realized why he had been unable to feel the relief he should at finding out Tate had murdered Martin Garland. His sense of guilt for that killing had not resided completely within himself. Part of it had attached itself to Quintin. Somehow Quintin had come to symbolize Blacklaws's fear of his own anger. Perhaps this fear had some of its roots in the deep antagonism which had lain between the men from the first. Most of it must have stemmed from the fact that Quintin was Martin's son and was so inextricably involved with all that had led up to the killing. For Blacklaws, coming back to Quintin, was like coming back to Martin all over again. Now that symbol was smashed. He had proved to himself that he could meet Quintin without the recurrence of what had happened with Martin. Freed of the sense of guilt for Martin's death, he had been able to fight Quintin without the rage he had so feared.

With this uplifting him, Blacklaws left his shack and took the river road to the Manatte house. A few miles south of Copper Bluffs he met King Wallace, rattling down the road in his cut-under wagon. The man pulled up and slacked out long and angular in the seat, offering Blacklaws a chew.

Blacklaws declined. "What's new in town, King?"

King cheeked his tobacco. "Big cut of Sharp's cattle run off near midnight. Roman's in town yelling for Sheridan to round up a posse."

Blacklaws spoke with a quiet restraint. "Was Sallier with Roman?"

"The Creole?" King frowned judiciously. "Can't rec'llect seeing him."

"Where was the rustling?"

"Over near Mexican Creek."

"Heading right into the thicket?"

"Where else? Nobody's ever going to find that packery. Might as well turn Jefferson County over to the rustlers."

Blacklaws changed the subject. It was weather and cotton crops and flood season for a few minutes, and then King took up his reins and bid Blacklaws good bye. Blacklaws waited till the man was out of sight then cut off the road, turning back in the same direction Wallace had taken. He pushed through timber and bog till he judged he was south of the slower-moving wagon and out of Wallace's sight, then he turned back onto the road.

He knew the ride he would have to make would be a terrible drain on Tar Baby, but it had to be done. He reached the New Orleans cattle trail, turned west. He passed the cutoff to his shack, kept going along the trail. He kept Tar Baby alternately cantering and trotting now. The spring sun drew a heavy yellow lather out of the horse that his pace did not allow to dry.

He was an hour and a half west of the Sabine when he reached Mexican Creek. The trail south along the creek was a poor one but, if the rustling had been done near this creek, it was the waterway they would use to drive in the cattle. And, if the rustling had taken place near midnight, they wouldn't have reached the coast much before now. Driving a herd of cattle through this swampland was a slow job, even when you pushed them, and the rustlers would have wasted a couple of hours building that false trail into the Big Thicket to throw off the posse. They wouldn't hit the coast much ahead of Blacklaws.

He headed south, through a tangled woodland of moss-hung cypresses that ringed swamps choked with pale hyacinth. He did not bother to cut sign on the banks of the creek. He had a good idea where the cattle would be brought out of the water. He had been riding well over two hours when he reached the first salt-grass prairies. The steers grazing across these open flats bore the Double Sickle brand on their gaunt hips.

At last the stench reached him. It was like rotten eggs, borne fitfully on the Gulf breeze. It was the rank odor of slaughter and of death, and it put Tar Baby to fiddling fretfully beneath him. The creek turned away, and the trail topped a rise and brought Blacklaws into view of the sea and of the Roman house.

It sat proudly on the bluff to his left, overlooking the Gulf. Directly beneath the house stood the slaughter shanties, the corrals, and the huge vats encrusted with dirty white brine where the tallow was rendered. Just west of these vats the dunes began, a tumbled labyrinth of sand and pickle grass, crisscrossed with the stagnant green fingers of water that probed in from the lagoons farther west.

The road curling down from the house ran through a cove of timber before it turned out on the flats and reached the pens. Blacklaws approached though this timber, keeping hidden from the house above, crossed the road where it was covered by the trees, and dismounted in the last fringe of stunted oaks. The sand dunes blocked off his view of the shanties and pens, but he could hear the plaintive bawl of cattle.

He moved westward till the road turned away from him and finally reached the dunes, where they were out of sight of the house. He ground hitched Tar Baby here and moved into the first sandy trough between two dunes. Some of the gulches were filled with stagnant water, and he was dripping ooze by the time he again came into sight of the outbuildings. He was looking at them from the west now, and this time it was the long slaughter shanties that blocked him off from the pens. If he moved any nearer the ocean, he would lose the cover of the dunes and be visible to the house. He crouched against the sloping side of a dune, studying the shanties. There was no sign of men. If they felt safe enough to leave the cattle in the pens without slaughtering and skinning immediately, they might also feel safe enough to go up to the house for breakfast and a rest after their grueling ride.

Blacklaws did not care about rounding up the rustlers now. He had no official capacity to make arrests, and it would be a foolish move for one man to try and get the whole bunch of them now, anyway. It might well ruin the whole thing. For he doubted if all the rustlers were here at the present time. All he wanted was definite word he could take back to Sheridan. Then the place could be staked out by enough men to handle the whole bunch of rustlers without a slip-up.

So the figuring was over. It was the same way it had been down there at Chenière Dominique when he had come to the end of what he could do with his mind and had been forced to take all the questions and answers in his two hands and see how they came out. He wanted a look at those cattle. It was as simple as that. And he could not do it without taking a chance. There were ten feet of open flats between this last dune and the first long shanty. Once in there he could move through to the other end and see the pens. He waited another long space, looking for fresh sign, for some indication that anyone was down there. The sullen surf boomed, hidden from him by the remaining dunes. A black-capped tern swung above, crying raucously. The wind carried spray into his face. There was no other sound. No other movement.

He took a last look at the house. Then he stood up and took four long strides to the slaughter shanty, swinging open the door and stepping in. It was gloomy inside and rank with the stench of blood and rotten meat. Sides of beef hung on hooks from the flimsy rafters, and there was a pile of bloody hides at the far end. He went down there, checking the brand on one. It was the Double Sickle.

The door at this end was open. He squinted his eyes against the fine dust raised by the cattle in the yonder pens. The brand on their hips was Harry Sharp's Dollar Sign.

"Don't turn around, Blacklaws," said a man from behind. "Just take out your gun, drop it, and kick it out the door."

Little muscles kinked up all across his back. He recognized the cynical drawl. It was Lee Deff. He finally lifted his Remington from its holster, dropped it, and gave it a kick.

"Get it now, Phil," said Deff.

In a moment Phil Manatte appeared in front of Blacklaws, outside the shanty. He stood staring at Blacklaws with a surprised hurt in his eyes. Finally he gave a little shake of his head and bent to pick up the Remington. When he straightened with the gun, his lips were tight. Blacklaws saw that there was still a heavy bandage on the boy's wounded shoulder, and his face was gaunt and pale. Blacklaws turned to see Deff coming down from the other end of the shed. He made a tall silhouette against the open door behind him, his Ward-Burton held in the crook of an elbow. He moved in a loose-jointed walk, his weather-grained face narrow and suspicious.

"Funny how things work," he said. "We was eating breakfast up in the house when Sallier saw the surf pulling one of the dories off. He sent us down to get it back on shore. Wouldn't have seen you at all but for that boat."

Blacklaws wanted to kick himself for not watching the shore more closely. That was the one place he had not expected any of them to be at this time.

"I guess we better go upstairs," Deff said.

The dust of the road ruffled beneath their feet like fine powder. Deff walked behind, but Phil came up beside Blacklaws, breathing hard with the climb.

"How's the wound, Phil?" asked Blacklaws.

"Kenny . . . ," began Phil, raising his hand in a vague protest. Then he dropped it helplessly, looking down at the road. "Taking time to heal, I guess," he said.

"How'd you get in this, Phil? Trying to convince Corsica those stocks were still paying off?"

Phil looked up in surprise. Finally he shook his head. "I had to, Kenny. Those stocks were all that was holding us together. If she found out they were worthless, it would break her."

"You underestimate your sister," Blacklaws said. He sent Phil a sidelong glance. "How deep you in it, kid?"

"That job I got shot on was my second time out," Phil said.

"That's not very deep," Blacklaws told him. "The law might not be hard on you, considering the circumstances. Ever hear of state's evidence? They give you a break for that."

"Take it easy, Blacklaws," Deff warned.

They walked on up the road, with Phil rubbing his

wounded shoulder, but a new expression had entered his face.

"Roman told me what Gauche and Agate did to you at Mock's, trying to find out where I was," he said.

"I thought Roman was after you for the rustling at the time," Blacklaws said. "I didn't know you were working for him."

"It doesn't matter what you thought." There was a puzzled wonder in the boy's eyes. "Roman said they tortured you."

Blacklaws's grin was flat. "They were starting to put the screws on, I guess."

"Why did you hold out, Kenny? Why didn't you tell?"

"I didn't want Roman to hand you over to the sheriff, Phil."

"But you knew I was a hide rustler by that time."

"I wasn't sure, Phil, and . . . you were still my friend."

"Yeah." Phil looked at him a moment, then he dropped his eyes to the road. "Remember how you used to try and teach me that hooley-ann?"

"You were pretty young to learn roping, Phil."

"I could have got it better if you'd stayed. Never nobody to take the time with me the way you did." He looked up sharply and then turned back to Deff. "Listen, Lee, you can't just. . . ."

"Just what?" Deff asked. They had reached the dooryard, and he halted, rifle still cradled in one elbow. "What Blacklaws saw out in the pen could hang us all, if he ever told," the man said. Then he squinted at Phil. "You ain't thinking of putting up a fight for an old friend?"

"Listen. . . ."

"You listen, kid," said Deff with fatherly cynicism. "You'd just foul everything up if you tried to get Blacklaws out of this. You're too damn' weak to start gunning at us. Even if you got the drop and pulled Blacklaws out, do you think you could last, with that shoulder? We'd be right on your tail. You'd hold Blacklaws down so much we couldn't help but get him. And do you think he'd leave you? You'd just make him dead meat for sure.''

The truth of this made its imprint in Phil's face, drawing a haggard look of defeat into his eyes. His shoulders dropped, and he threw a helpless glance to Blacklaws.

''You better get back down and see if anybody else is coming, kid,'' said Deff. ''And remember, it's your neck as well as ours.''

Phil turned to go down the road, but Blacklaws had caught a faint flash in the boy's eyes as they sent a momentary glance northward. He hoped he was right about what that meant. Phil might be too weak with his wound to put up a fight and get away with Blacklaws, but there was still a chance of riding for help. He wouldn't even have to go clear into Copper Bluffs. One of Obermeier's line shacks was up on the fringe of Congo Bog. Then Blacklaws felt a defeat of his own. Maybe Phil didn't want to help him that badly.

He turned inside at a wave of Deff's gun. Afternoon shadows softened the squalor of cracked mirrors and fallen plaster. Blacklaws went through the entrance hall and into the living room ahead of Deff. He stopped within the door at sight of Mock Fannin, sitting on the couch. Mock came forward in his surprise, hanging there on the edge of the couch, and the two of them stared emptily at each other. Blacklaws felt a vague sickness.

''I should have listened to you,'' he said. ''The only time in your life you told the truth. John Roman and a thousand hides a day and a hundred thousand dollars a year.''

There was a protest in the way Mock's slack mouth

parted, but he did not say anything. Finally he settled back on the couch, still gazing helplessly at Blacklaws. The other man in the room was Gauche Sallier, lounging indolently against the mantel, ironic amusement in his sooty eyes.

"Blacklaws was down by the pens," Deff told the Creole. "He saw the Dollar Sign stuff."

"Roman should have let me finish with you up there at Mock's," Sallier murmured.

"We better wait till Roman comes back," Deff said.

Sallier nodded at the wing chair. Blacklaws went over and sat down. Mock got up from the couch and ambled to the sideboard where a decanter of whiskey stood.

"I'm going to get drunk," he said.

Deff put his rifle against the wall and built himself a smoke. Then he walked to the French windows and stood looking out, drawing deeply. Mock stayed by the sideboard, drinking steadily. Whenever he met Blacklaws's glance, there was a strange, twisted look in his eyes. Blacklaws looked at Deff's rifle at the door and realized how useless the thought was. Sallier would welcome the chance to cut him down.

The shadows lengthened. There was an increasing constriction in Blacklaws's chest. It bothered his breathing at first. The men shifted restlessly around the room. Time became a palpable thing. Blacklaws could almost feel it running out between his fingers. He had never realized before how precious it could be.

It was late afternoon when Roman came. The road trembled to drumming hoofs, and the voices swelled up outside. There was the creak of saddle leather, and Roman's shout as he came into the entrance way.

"Gauche, you here? Everything went like a Swiss watch. Innes made a trail into the thicket with what Dollar Sign stuff you left him. I pushed Sheridan and Obermeier along till they were so deep in the thicket they almost didn't find their way out. I figured I gave you enough time to get here.''

He had reached the door from the entrance hall to the living room, with the others coming in behind him. His hoarse voice cut off at the sight of Blacklaws. Agate Ayers and Eddie Hyde and two other riders banked up behind him, the clatter of their boots dying before them.

"Deff found him down on the flats checking the Dollar Sign stuff," Sallier explained.

Roman stared at Blacklaws, a little flutter of muscle rippling his whiskey-veined jowls. "Who you working for, Kenny?" he said at last.

"What does it matter?" Blacklaws answered.

Roman studied him a moment longer. Then he stamped viciously across the room, past Blacklaws, to the side table. Mock solemnly poured him a drink. Roman took it neat, wiping the back of a dirty hand across his mouth. He let his breath out in a tired wheeze.

"I should have known it," he said. "All the stock dicks in the state chasing around for years and not a bobble. Then you come back and figure it all out with that head of yours in a few weeks. The sheriff couldn't've brought you back. Was it Charlie Carew? Feature that! The head of the Jefferson Association doesn't even know when his own detectives bring in a man to expose him." He snorted ruefully. "How long you known it was me?"

"Not till today, for sure," Blacklaws said, realizing there was no use at pretense. "It came together in pieces. First it was Garland, claiming to have something on you that would let the rustlers operate without interference from you. I couldn't figure out why the rustlers didn't get in touch with Garland. The only logical answer was that what Garland had was no good . . . or that you were with the rustlers. Then Phil told me about the wet-blanket job Garland had found with your brand on the outside and the old Quarter Moon on the inside.'' Blacklaws looked up at Roman. ''Why didn't you let Garland know it was useless?''

Roman grinned. ''Garland thought he could gain more out of what he had by selling it to the rustlers than by turning it over to the law. As long as I kept him thinking that, he wouldn't give it to the law.'' He sobered. ''But that was only part of the picture. What completed it?''

''I cut sign of a couple of rustlings,'' Blacklaws said. ''I saw how you were leaving a phony trail into the thicket and running the bulk of the stuff off in water. Then I found out Sallier was never with you when you were in town raising a ruckus. I figured he was the one running the cattle while you were throwing everybody off the trail.''

Roman was staring into his empty glass again, talking almost to himself. ''I couldn't've done it any other way, Kenny. Look at them going down. Obermeier used to be the kingpin around here. He's about through. Sharp will be next. The only reason I'm still able to operate is I've kept up enough volume of hides and tallow to make it pay off. I couldn't have done that with just my own herds.''

''I wasn't actually sure it was you till today,'' Blacklaws said. ''It didn't surprise me. A man who was capable of branding through a wet blanket in the old days would be capable of rustling hides now.''

Roman's head lifted, blood darkening his face. ''You know how we get rid of spoiled beef here, Kenny? We drag it out to the end of the pier and dump it off. Those sharks pick it so clean nobody'd ever find any remains.''

Blacklaws felt tension fill his body as he saw how his time had run out. Roman looked at Sallier. Then he turned to walk to the French windows, his back to the room. He stood there, staring out, and reached up to rub the back of his shaven neck in a vicious gesture.

"Damn you, Kenny. I wish you hadn't done this."

Sallier moved to the end of the couch, looking down at Blacklaws.

"Get up," he said. "We'll go down to the pier."

Chapter Twenty

A gossamer mist sometimes rose off the river in late afternoon to steal through the grove surrounding the Manatte house till the trees and underbrush had the blurred configurations of some ill-defined dream. The mist seemed to strangle sound, leaving only an eerie silence that would brook no intrusion. It was an unworldly time of day, when almost anything could happen. A strange time for Corsica Manatte to be standing out on the low bluffs, staring down at the river, her gingham dress clinging damply to her body. It seemed to her, as she stood there, that she had been standing there once before, in some other life, waiting for a rider to show up. And when he had come, it had not been the one she had expected.

She felt no surprise, therefore, when the horseman first appeared, down the road, a shadowy form, resolving itself only slowly as it approached.

"Dee?" she asked. The man did not answer, guiding his horse toward her at a walk, and then she recognized him. His name escaped her in a whisper. "Quintin."

He halted the Copperbottom beside her, staring down

with a strange expression on his face. His voice sounded unnatural. "You were expecting Dee?"

She felt her body rise toward him in a sharp fear as she saw the bruises on his face, the cut across his cheek. "Quintin," she said breathlessly. "You . . . and Kenny . . . ?"

He seemed to lift in the saddle, something acute and savage narrowing his face. He settled back slowly, without answering her, a ridge of white flesh forming around his compressed lips. He was looking beyond her, eyes squinted. Then she became aware of the saddlebags, loaded till they bulged, and the valise lashed on behind the cantle. The fear left her in a rush of understanding.

"You didn't kill him. You're leaving. He whipped you. You wouldn't be leaving unless he whipped you . . . !"

His eyes regained their focus on her.

"Listen, Corsica, he's nothing but a tinhorn detective, that's all he came back for. He didn't come back for you and, when he's through with this, he'll leave again. Why even think about him any more?"

For an instant the bitterness gave his voice its old vitality. He was leaning down, and she could see a flash in his eyes, but her own eyes were wide with comprehension.

"You did everything you could to stop him," she said. "You knew that out of all the men along the river he was the most likely to find the packery. And now that he's whipped you, he'll go on and find it. There isn't anything that can stop him. You know you're through. He's going to find it before you do, Quintin, and it's too late for you. That's it, isn't it?"

He leaned farther toward her. "Corsica, come away with me. Austin, Saint Louis, Chicago. Any of the big towns. I've told you how wonderful it was. . . ."

"You still don't understand, do you?" she said, with

the feeling she was speaking to him across a great distance.

That moment of bitter vitality drained slowly from him. The mist planted waxen shadows in the hollows of his cheeks, rendering his face desiccated and aged. The eyes lost their restless shine and took on a dark emptiness. He seemed about to speak again, but he did not. It seemed a long time before he took up the reins and turned his horse on down the road.

Watching him disappear into the mist, Corsica thought she had never seen such defeat in a man. *She could feel none of the anger, the scorn, she had known when she had first begun to see what he truly was. She felt a vague pity. And she wondered how she could have ever thought she was in love with him. She saw now how little passion there had been in her attraction for the man. It had taken Blacklaws, and the comparison of her feelings for him, to show her that. It almost frightened her now to realize that, if Blacklaws had not come back, she might have gone on thinking what she felt for Garland was love, and waiting for him to gain those glittering heights of ambition so they could marry.*

She turned back toward the house. *Now it was striking her as a strange irony that neither of the men had been killed. It had seemed that a killing was inevitable, that the intensity of antagonism between them would be satisfied by nothing less. Then she realized there was a truer justice this way. Blacklaws's triumph would have been hollow if he had been forced to kill Garland. It was the thing he had run from in the first place and to come back to it would only have deepened his own defeat. She realized it was what Blacklaws had gone out to meet last night. Only in meeting Garland, and not killing him, was Blacklaws's triumph complete.* It uplifted her, as she walked back down the drive and up onto the porch.

She was about to go inside when a movement out in

the grove caught her eye. She peered intently, trying to make out Dee. The motion became a man. He seemed to be veering and stumbling. She caught at a colonnette in horrified surprise as she recognized Tate.

His matted hair hung down over his face. His left hand was pressed tightly into the blood-soaked shirt over his ribs. In his other hand he held a Bowie knife. The creaking of Troy Manatte's rocker, at the end of the gallery, stopped.

"It's Tate," he said. "Looks like he's hurt."

"Dad!"—her voice came out with great difficulty—"get up, get inside quickly!"

"That's no kind of hospitality," Troy said. "Man's hurt. We've got to take care of him."

She whirled to run down the gallery, catching her father's arm. "Dad, don't you understand? Get up. Please . . . !"

The old man floundered to his feet, fighting her irascibly. They reached the end of the railing just as Tate came to the bottom of the steps. Troy pulled up here.

"Let go," he muttered. "This man needs help. Come on inside, Tate. My wife'll take care of you."

"Dad, please . . . !"

"Corsica, you're not being nice about this at all. How did it happen, Tate?"

"Waco Sheridan," said Tate in a hoarse voice, swaying there at the bottom of the steps. "Waco Sheridan and his deputy. They said they wanted me for Martin Garland's murder. You're the only one who could have told."

Troy frowned vaguely. "Martin ain't dead. I saw him not an hour ago."

"I should have come and got you a long time ago, but I thought your brains was all clabbered, and you couldn't remember anything any more. But you did, didn't you? You told 'em all about Martin Garland."

Corsica saw the veil shred across Troy's eyes. He touched his forehead in a vague, wondering way, looking beyond Tate. Suddenly he stiffened, voice shrill.

"Corsica, where's Sheridan? He said he'd protect me. I told you Tate would come!"

He pulled away from her. Fear made a parchment mask of his face. With a snarling sound, Tate began to come up the steps. Corsica moved in front of her father, backing toward the door after him.

"Tate," she pleaded. "You can't gain anything by doing this."

"I can pay him back. I can pay them all back." There was a delirious light in Tate's eyes. "You're as bad as the rest. Think you kin do anything to old Tate. You told 'em, Troy. I'll get you for it."

Corsica backed into the hall. Tate stumbled on the steps, fresh blood pumping through his fingers. He got up again, unsteadily, and staggered up the steps and across the gallery into the entrance hall, maneuvering between Corsica and the stairway with a darting motion.

"You won't get away," he gasped. "I'll kill you, Troy."

"Where are they?" said Troy in a shrill voice. "They promised they'd protect me."

With her own backing body, Corsica forced her father through the door into the parlor. She realized she was holding her breath and let it escape with a small sobbing sound. Tate's bloodshot eyes glittered wildly.

"You're crazy," she said. "You're as crazy as those razorbacks."

"That's what they all say," he panted. "Old Tate's crazy. Old Tate won't be able to do nothing. Take his hogs. Don't matter if his earmark's on 'em. Take 'em. Kill 'em. Kill him!"

He was bawling now, like a child in a tantrum, and he came at them in a rush. Corsica pushed Troy back with her hands held out wide. They knocked a chair over, and her father almost fell. Then they were up against the mantel. Tate stumbled on the fallen chair, caught at it to keep from falling. This stopped him a moment.

"Please, Tate, what do you hope to gain? He's an old man . . . ?"

"Ain't no use. Get out of the way, Corsica."

She spread her arms out backward around Troy, her whole body pressing against his trembling frame. "Please, don't . . . !"

"Then I'll kill you too," he gasped, straightening up from the chair and coming at her with the knife upraised.

"Tate!"

The shot smashed her cry. Tate's body lifted up with a sudden jerk. His mouth was pulled wide open with shock. Then he fell heavily against her and slid down, sprawling across the floor.

Corsica's eyes lifted slowly from his body till they found Phil, standing in the doorway, the smoking gun in his hand. Phil took a heavy breath, looking at his sister.

"What'd I walk in on?" he asked.

"Phil." His name left her feebly. "Oh, Phil. . . ."

Then she was shaking in reaction and staggering across Tate to drop in the wing chair. The tears began to squeeze soundlessly from her eyes, and she squinted them shut and sat shuddering deeply. She heard Phil move across the room, and his hand grasped her shoulder.

"It's all right, Corsica. Whatever it was, it's all over."

He got her a drink, forced her to take it. Only after she had quit sputtering did she notice the subdued urgency of his movements. She caught his hand, staring up at him.

207

"I sent Dee to Rouquette to take him to Mock's and bring you home," she said.

"I haven't been at Mock's in a long time," he told her wearily. He took his hand from hers and went over to the divan, sinking into it. "There's no time to waste, Corsica. I don't think I can go any farther. I was riding for the sheriff. I almost killed my horse and stopped here for a fresh one. It was right on the way. You've got to get to Sheridan somehow and tell him Blacklaws is down at Roman's. They're going to kill Kenny. Roman is the head of the hide rustlers, and Blacklaws has found it all out . . . !"

He broke off, turning toward the door. Corsica had been so intent upon what Phil was saying that she had not heard Sheridan come in. The sheriff made a tall, stooped shape in the doorway.

"We was on Tate's trail," he said, pursing his lips. "Looks like we come too late."

Phil lolled his head weakly back against the couch, breathing in a shallow way. "Did you hear what I said?"

"Most of it," said Sheridan. He went over to Tate and hunkered down beside him, rolling him over. "Dead. Guess that's the best way."

Phil leaned forward in a weak anger. "Sheriff, you have no time to waste. When did Roman leave you?"

"About an hour ago," Sheridan said. "We lost sign of those rustlers in the Big Thicket, but we picked up fresh sign of Tate and his hogs. We'd already tried to get Tate at his shack yesterday evening, but he wasn't there."

"If you left Roman an hour ago, he couldn't have gotten to his place yet," Phil said. "Please, Sheridan, won't you take my word and try to save Kenny?"

Sheridan studied Phil from those wise, crow-tracked

eyes, pouting studiously. Then he hitched at his cartridge belt.

"Sure, Phil. We'll go."

Corsica rose. "I'll go with you."

"Now, Corsica," Sheridan said, "you can't make a ride like that. We'll be pushing for all we're worth."

"You start ahead," she said. "I'll get on my habit. My horse will pick you up. Phil can stay with Dad."

"Nobody has to stay with me," Troy broke in. He went around Tate without seeing him and walked shakily to the door. "Tell your ma I'm getting my gear." He turned and smiled vaguely at them. "It'll be a good night to work that new stud of mine."

Chapter Twenty-One

The muffled cannons of the surf boomed in their endless siege of the shore, drowning the raucous cries of the black-capped terns that hovered over the dunes. A wind was rising to carry the spray far in over the lagoons. Blacklaws narrowed his eyes against its faint sting. His high-heeled boots made a crunching passage through the sand, leading him inexorably toward that rickety pier.

"Let's turn through this way," Agate Ayers said.

They rounded the tip of a dune, tousled with pickle grass, and walked down the edge of stagnant water that filled the trough. A lot of things were going through Blacklaws's mind. He was thinking of Corsica, and their lovemaking in the line shack. He was thinking of her face. Her body partially naked and how it had felt to his touch. Of how he wished he had seen her this morning. Just one more time. Even a glimpse. And he was thinking that he couldn't let them do this without trying something. Even though he knew it would be useless.

"This way, now, *m'sieu*."

The trail turned off the arm of water into the sandy bottom between two more dunes. Instead of following the wagon road, they had cut off onto a footpath that led more directly to the pier. The shanties and vats and pens were to their left now. Over the nearing explosion of surf, the mournful bawling of cattle was audible.

"Through here now."

Another turn, into another trough between dunes, brought them into direct sight of the surf, with its roar no longer muffled by intervening land. Blacklaws was half way through when he thought he heard another faint sound somewhere. He could not be sure. They were almost to the end of these dunes when Mock spoke from behind.

"Hold it, Sallier, Ayers, and drop your guns. I've got seventeen of my own cutters looking down your briskets."

Blacklaws stopped and wheeled. Surprise still left Agate's mouth open. Sallier's narrow black head was half way turned. At the other end of the dunes Blacklaws saw Mock, a drunken grin spread into his greasy cheeks. Agate's gun had been holstered, and he pulled it out to drop it. Sallier finally let his go from his hand. That intense, womanish anger was whitening his face.

"Get their cutters and hurry up, Kenny," Mock said. "Roman stepped out a minute and gave me a chance to leave. He must have found I'm gone by now. Where's your horse?"

Blacklaws was already scooping up Sallier's gun. "Back across the road in those trees."

"Come on, then. We'll go that way."

Blacklaws got Agate's gun and dropped it in his holster and then ran for Mock. The bowlegged man turned and splashed knee deep into an arm of the lagoon. Blacklaws ran through reeds and pickle grass and into the water after him. He flung a look back to see Sallier cutting across the top of the dune toward the pens. Agate had his hands cupped to his mouth and was calling.

"Roman, they're getting away! Mock got Blacklaws away from us!"

The labyrinth of grassed-over dunes closed around Blacklaws and Mock, cutting off sight of Agate behind them and muffling his voice. They ran down an aisle between ridges of sand till a third dune blocked them off. They turned down the flank of this dune, coming to more water, slogging through, emerging with the ooze splashing off of them. They followed this zigzag path through another series of troughs. Instead of turning aside from the next dune that flung itself across their way, Mock scrambled right up its side. He was at the top, when a shout came from somewhere beyond and the sharp crack of a gun.

Mock's breath left him in a gasp of pain. He remained skylighted above Blacklaws another moment. Then he pitched off on the other side.

Blacklaws knew it would be foolish to go on over the top, if they had already picked off Mock that way, but he couldn't leave Mock. He saw that this dune petered out ten yards to his right, leaving an opening between it and the next hump of sand. He ran down that way, boots sinking deeply, till he reached its end. Then he crouched against the sandy slope and worked around the tip till he could see down the trough on the other side.

This was where Mock should have tumbled, but he was not in sight. There was a trail of blood in the sand. It led through an opening between two other dunes.

That's not the road, thought Blacklaws. *He's trying to lead them away from me with that trail of blood.*

"Deff . . . ?" called Roman. It was so near it shocked Blacklaws. "Deff, where are you?"

"Over here toward the pens. We got him between us. Sallier's coming in from the beach side. He went to the shed for another gun, I think."

"I put Ernie and Peele in the timber across the road," said Roman. "He won't make it over there."

"Roman?" It was Agate's voice from farther off. "Where are you? I haven't got a gun."

"Over this way." It was Deff who answered. "You can have my six-gun. I've got my Ward-Burton. We hit Mock."

"Hear that, Kenny?" shouted Roman. "You're all alone now. We've got you pinched off. Come on out."

The hell with you, Roman.

"Come on out, Kenny. We'll talk it over."

The hell you will.

No sound came after that. No sound of voices, anyway, or of men. Only the sea, the birds, the wind sighing across the dunes. Blacklaws saw how exposed he was here. Behind him he caught sight of a dead-end trough. That would be his best chance. He could make his stand with his back at the dead end. They'd have to skylight themselves coming over the top to get him, from behind or from either side. They'd have to come into the open to get him from the front end. He worked his way through deep sand to the dry gulch between dunes and to its end, where it backed into the box end.

Then he stood there, his clothes wet with sweat, the wind-blown sand grimy on his face. *Waiting was always the hardest. It took him back to all the other times he had waited. The three days he'd spent in the loft of that barn in Wyoming, waiting for Reardon. That seemed like another lifetime. Or the night in the back room of the*

*saloon at Deadwood. Or the cave up in the Wind Rivers.
Had he felt this way? This dryness in his throat. This
strange need for more air.*

*At least I won't have to move. That's what saved me
in the loft. Reardon was moving, and I wasn't. The eye
picks up movement quicker than shape. It let me see him
a fraction of a second before he saw me. And I won't
have to move now. . . .*

Sallier appeared suddenly in the open end of the
trough. He whirled with sight of Blacklaws, surprise
making a gaping hole of his mouth. Blacklaws fired before the Creole could. It knocked dust from Sallier's
shirt across his belly and drove him backward like a
sharp blow. He thrust one leg behind to keep from falling and tried to line up his gun again. Blacklaws fired a
second time. This time the dust kicked out of the Creole's chest, and he pitched over backward into the sand.
At the same time Roman's shout broke out.

"Somebody's got him over here, Agate . . . !"

He came up over the top of the dune like a charging
bull, right above Blacklaws. Blacklaws had to flop onto
his back against the slope and shoot directly above his
head. It struck Roman fully in his great belly, jerking
him forward so hard his own bullet drove into sand
above Blacklaws's head. The sand spewed into Blacklaws's eyes, blinding him. He fired the second time with
his eyes tightly squinted, unable to see Roman. He heard
the man grunt, and then the immense weight of him
crashed down on top of Blacklaws.

It tore Blacklaws away from the slope and twisted him
around to roll into the bottom of the trough with Roman
on top. It knocked all the wind out of him, and he lay
there a moment gasping for air. He had lost his gun in
the fall, but he had Agate's gun in his holster. He tried
to squirm out from beneath Roman's great dead weight.
His right arm was still pinned against his side, and the

213

gun with it, when Agate appeared at the open end of the trough. He had Deff's six-shooter and raised it upon sight of Blacklaws.

At the same time Mock appeared over the top of the dunes at the dead end of the trough. His gun made a smashing sound. It spun Agate around and spilled him back against the slope of the dune. He lay sprawled there against the pickle grass, staring at the gun that had been knocked six feet from him.

"Don't do it," Mock said. "I never miss when I'm drunk."

Agate slid down to a sitting position, grabbing his bloody right shoulder, spitting disgustedly. "Ain't that a sack of hell?"

Mock slid down into the trough, grinning broadly. "Guess they thought I cashed in my chips when they saw me take the dive. I figured it was best to let them go on believing that. It only hit me in the calf. Never saw so much blood."

"Deff's still around with those other two," said Blacklaws, now out from beneath Roman.

"Let's drag the corpse up on top," Mock told him. "Maybe it'll take the tucker out of them."

It was heavy labor to get the immense dead man on top of the hump. Then, leaving him sprawled there, they slid back down, and Blacklaws called out.

"Deff? Roman's dead."

"The hell you say."

"On top of the dune. Stand up and take a look. We won't shoot."

They couldn't see him stand up. The long silence was eloquent. Mock wiped his mouth, leaving greasy white finger tracks in the flesh of his unshaven jowls.

"They aren't the kind to stick when the game's over like that. They'll be lighting a shuck now. Do you care?"

"We know who they are. They'll be picked up sooner or later." Blacklaws turned to Mock. "Maybe you'd better do the same thing."

Mock's eyebrows raised. "You wouldn't let the leader get away?"

"The leader?"

Mock made a disgusted motion toward Roman. "He was just the front. I was the main wheel. This isn't my only packery. I got 'em strung all the way from here. . . ."

"Sure, sure, a thousand hides and a hundred tons of lard a day."

"You don't believe me?"

"I don't think you ever rustled a hide in your life. You figured out I was hunting for the rustlers when you found me on Chenière Dominique. If you'd been with Roman, you'd have told him then. He didn't know a thing about it. He was surprised as a cow with a pink calf when he came in and found out I was a cattle dick today."

"Kenny. . . ."

"You just knew Phil wouldn't be safe at home. You brought him down here that day Sheridan began getting close. Roman gave you the choice of getting fed to the sharks or working with them. He probably thought he'd added a prime member to his gang when he got the most disreputable bushwhacker in Jefferson County to join up."

A hurt look filled Mock's dissolute face. "Why will nobody ever believe me?"

"I believe you. I'll have to tell Sheridan I had the biggest hide rustler of them all right in my hands, and he got away. My arm was so numb from being pinned under Roman I couldn't get my gun out in time when you skedaddled. Now buy that trunk, you damned old

215

scalawag. If Phil rode for the sheriff, they'll be here soon.''

Mock shook his head sadly and walked to the end of the trough. Here he stopped, looking back at Blacklaws, and the bland grin broke across his face.

''War bag all laced up, Kenny?''

''All laced up, Mock.''

After the man's squat, bowlegged figure had disappeared amid the dunes, Blacklaws, with Agate marching in front, got Tar Baby from the timber and led her up the road. They went up to the house. It was night now, and Blacklaws lit the hog-fat candles on the mantel and sideboards and tended to Agate's arm. Then Sheridan and Corsica and the others came up to the porch with a great stamping of horses and calling. Blacklaws answered them. Corsica was the first to come bursting into the room, filmed with dust and beaten down by the ride but glowing with a great relief at sight of him.

''There's a cut of Dollar Sign stuff down in the pens,'' Blacklaws told Sheridan. ''It ought to constitute the evidence you want. Roman and Sallier are down there. Dead. The rest got away, but I can give you their names.''

''I'll leave Cameron here with Agate and go down and take a look,'' Sheridan said. He gave a pouting smile at what was passing between Corsica and Blacklaws. ''Why don't you two go out on the gallery while I'm gone? It's nice out there.''

Light from the windows cast lemon rectangles across the flagstones of the porch. Blacklaws led Corsica through these to the cool shadows beyond. They had been holding back, in the presence of the others. Now she came into his arms with a long sighing sound. The feel of her body against him was ripeness and excitement and fulfillment all in one.

"I was riding up to tell you something when this broke," he said at last.

"I saw Quintin." Her voice was muffled against his chest. "He was leaving."

Blacklaws was silent for a moment. "I guess that's the best way, isn't it? That's what I wanted to tell you, Corsica."

"I know. . . ." She lifted her face to his, her voice swelling eagerly. "You're free now, Kenny. The symbol of Quintin is smashed. You don't have to be afraid of what you feel ever again."

"No," he said. "Never again."

Her lips were cool against his at first, then they gained warmth and passion and, though he had been back in the land of his birth for many weeks, only now did he truly feel that he had come home.

About the Author

Les Savage, Jr. was an extremely gifted writer who was born in Alhambra, California, but grew up in Los Angeles. His first published story was "Bullets and Bullwhips" accepted by the prestigious Street & Smith's *Western Story Magazine*. Almost ninety more magazine stories all set on the American frontier followed, many of them published in Fiction House magazines such as *Frontier Stories* and *Lariat Story Magazine* where Savage became a superstar with his name on many covers. His first novel, *Treasure of the Brasada*, appeared in 1947, the first of twenty-four published novels to appear in the next decade. Due to his preference for historical accuracy, Savage often ran into problems with book editors in the 1950s who were concerned about marriages between his protagonists and women of different races— a commonplace on the real frontier but not in much Western fiction in that decade. As a result of the censorship imposed on many of his works, only now have they been fully restored by returning to the author's original manuscripts. *Table Rock*, published in 1993 in the United States by Walker and Company, in 1994 in the United Kingdom by Robert Hale, Ltd., and available in full-length audio from Books on Tape, was Savage's last book, initially suppressed by his agent in part because of its sympathetic depiction of Chinese on the frontier. More recently *Fire Dance at Spider Rock* and *Medicine Wheel* have appeared.

Savage died young, at thirty-five, from complications arising out of hereditary diabetes and elevated cholesterol. However, his considerable legacy lives after him, there to reach a new generation of readers. His reputation as one of the finest authors of Western and frontier fiction continues and is winning new legions of admirers, both in the United States and abroad. Such noteworthy titles as *Silver Street Woman, Return to Warbow*, and *Beyond Wind River* have become classics of Western fiction. *Return to Warbow* is one of four of his novels so far to have appeared as a major motion picture.

LES SAVAGE, JR.
MEDICINE WHEEL

Bob Hogarth arrives in Wyoming's Big Horn Basin with nothing but a small herd of cattle, the result of stubborn scraping and saving back in Texas. He is determined to do better, to own his own ranch, to become a man of substance. But there are lots of folks who aren't too eager to see Hogarth succeed, other ranchers with their own plans for the future, and a mysterious rustler on a barefoot horse. Nobody told Hogarth his dreams would come easy . . . but he knows they are worth fighting for.

___4444-7 $4.50 US/$5.50 CAN

SPUR AWARD-WINNING AUTHOR

GORDON D. SHIRREFFS

Southwest Drifter. Wes Yardigan's luck is beginning to run dry. It kept him alive all the years he's drifted the territory, a stubborn saddle tramp chasing the wind. Now he wants to settle down, and has even managed to scratch up a stake—just in time for the Indians to sweep down out of the hills and leave him with nothing but his own thick skin. One more day in this blistering country and he won't even have that. But Yardigan's luck hasn't quite run out. Two men ride in with a curious proposition—a deal that will give him a chance to stake himself again. And after he agrees, he realizes he should have taken his chances in the desert.

_4207-X $3.99 US/$4.99 CAN

HIGHPOCKETS

DOUGLAS SAVAGE

In the autumn of his days, Highpockets stumbles upon a half-frozen immigrant boy, nearly dead and terrified after being separated from his family's wagon train. For one long, brutal winter Highpockets tries to teach the boy all he needs to know to survive in a land as dangerous as it is beautiful. But will it be enough to see both man and boy through the deadly trial that is still to come?

___4400-5 $3.99 US/$4.99 CAN

DANGER RIDGE
TIM McGUIRE

Clay Cole is a man with a shadowy past. Most folks know he is good with a gun, but that is all they know. Very few know the Army is out to court-martial him for something he didn't do. And even fewer know he has accepted a job to lead a young bride along a dangerous trail to meet her husband. But the men who do know it are aiming to kill him and the woman along the trail. And the easiest place to do that is the treacherous sort few men make it through—the place the Westerners call danger ridge.

___4410-2 $4.50 US/$5.50 CAN

Dorchester Publishing Co., Inc.
P.O. Box 6640
Wayne, PA 19087-8640

Please add $1.75 for shipping and handling for the first book and $.50 for each book thereafter. NY, NYC, and PA residents, please add appropriate sales tax. No cash, stamps, or C.O.D.s. All orders shipped within 6 weeks via postal service book rate. Canadian orders require $2.00 extra postage and must be paid in U.S. dollars through a U.S. banking facility.

Name_____
Address_____
City_____ State_____ Zip_____
I have enclosed $_____ in payment for the checked book(s).
Payment <u>must</u> accompany all orders. ☐ Please send a free catalog.
    CHECK OUT OUR WEBSITE! www.dorchesterpub.com